VINTAGE

A HOUSE OF RAIN AND SNOW

Srijato, one of the most celebrated Bengali poet-lyricists of our times, received the Ananda Puroskar in 2004 for his book *Udanta Sawb Joker* (All Those Flying Jokers).

Maharghya Chakraborty is a well-known translator. He teaches at St Xavier's College, Kolkata.

T0158488

Celebrating 35 Years of
Penguin Random House India

A
HOUSE
OF RAIN
AND
SNOW

SRIJATO

Translated from the Bengali by
MAHARGHYA CHAKRABORTY

VINTAGE
An imprint of Penguin Random House

VINTAGE

USA | Canada | UK | Ireland | Australia
New Zealand | India | South Africa | China | Singapore

Vintage is part of the Penguin Random House group of companies
whose addresses can be found at global.penguinrandomhouse.com

Published by Penguin Random House India Pvt. Ltd
4th Floor, Capital Tower 1, MG Road,
Gurugram 122 002, Haryana, India

First published in Vintage by Penguin Random House India 2023

ISBN 9780143459804

Typeset in Adobe Garamond Pro by MAP Systems, Bengaluru, India

www.penguin.co.in

'Remembrance of things past is not necessarily the remembrance of things as they were.'

—Marcel Proust

A Confession

It often happens that we cannot come to terms with the reality of time that has gone by. It seems like a distant dream or perhaps an echo of a past life. Like something that has almost no connection with our present situation or even with the person we are now. But if it is so unfamiliar, then why does it not let go of us? Why does it chase us around like a stubborn draught? Today, it seems to me there is only one reason why this happens. Memory. Between the past and the future, between reality and the unreal, between this life and the ones before, it is memory that remains like a bridge shrouded in mist, a steadfast thread that cannot be broken or undone. So, from time to time, along that bridge, clinging to that thread, memories of our past lives and the times we have left behind find their way into the pages of the present. Like divers coming up for air after being underwater for a long time.

There is not much that I have to say about this book. It's rather amusing to try and look back at one's past from a safe distance. This tale has a significant portion of my growing-up years sewn into its very fabric, something that has not been so apparent in my previous novels. I am a firm believer that there's no writing that is not autobiographical. For any writer, every one of their works contains traces of their own lives, like every star in the cosmos contains traces of the Big Bang. Writing brings together this truth, these memories, along with our dreams and imagination. This confluence is like holding up a mirror to our familiar lives, to come face to face with an ever-so-slightly unrecognizable person on the other side. This book contains that confluence too. The only difference is that once I was done writing, it didn't take me long to recognize the person standing in the midst of it all.

Writing a novel requires certain specific kinds of investments, much like gambling. These investments have to be made without considering the returns and without thinking about victory and defeat. These obviously include love, time, labour and so on, but more than that, it demands enduring an extraordinary amount of pain. It requires a certain steadfastness and honesty about oneself, one's truth, one's life and surroundings. It's definitely not an easy task, hence it's strangely addictive. It's an addiction for pain and sorrow and, over and above everything else, an obsession with self-discovery. I have had to dig deep within myself for this book, whose scars I must bear for a very long time. That's because there are certain things that lie dormant in us which are best left undisturbed. But if one has to stand in front of that aforementioned mirror, then some things and some actions become inevitable.

There are those to whom I owe an immense debt of gratitude. At the forefront is Penguin Random House, especially Premanka Goswami, without whose tireless efforts and enthusiasm I doubt this book would have ever happened. I must acknowledge my translator, Maharghya Chakraborty, who has spent an immense amount of time and energy in creating such a fantastic translation of my novel. I deeply appreciate designer Gunjan Ahlawat, whose cover design has a deep resonance with my writing. And last but definitely not least, my favourite poet and lyricist Gulzarji, who not only managed to read my novel despite his packed schedule but also gave his valuable comments. Without all of them, this book would never have seen the light of day.

Finally, there's something I must confess. Never before after finishing a book have I felt this complete and yet this empty. This is an inexplicable feeling; I have no name for it. As if the very day I suddenly chanced upon an old photo album, I also lost all my old, invaluable letters safely hidden away in a box. It is this mix of wholeness and lack that I leave with my readers. The only things I will keep for myself are a secret notebook; the roads of old Kolkata; a lonely, time-worn milkwood tree and a pair of windows, with rain outside one and snow outside the other.

Srijato

1

It rains outside one of the windows, snows outside the other. This happens in Pushkar's house. Well, not their house exactly, they are tenants, but this does happen there. Not every day, only from time to time. No one other than Pushkar knows about this, neither does he wish to tell anyone. There are two windows in his room, side by side, one almost touching the other. Outside one of them it rains the entire day and snows throughout outside the other. On the days this happens, Pushkar finds himself unable to leave the house.

The light in rented houses has a pallor of its own, a unique dimness, as if it never wishes to fully brighten. As if it knows it has been confined within the walls of a leased property. So every evening it flickers into life in a blurry, understated manner. Like it lacks self-confidence, lacks the courage to be loud. Thus the walls of the rented property, the calendar hanging on it, the door that refuses to shut properly and the ancient curtain sticking to it—they all look a bit pale in that low, dim light.

This is not a lie, Pushkar is well aware of that. It is hardly possible to know how one's house looks from within. Like one has to be in space to truly understand how the earth looks, one has to step out of one's house to see it, from afar. Pushkar has never really managed to do it that much. There's a narrow lane just outside their house and rows and rows of walls and houses of the tiny neighbourhood beyond it. He has never managed to examine his house from a distance. So one must wonder how he figured out the matter of the paleness of the lights. It was quite easy. Whenever he had to take the local train back from a friend's distant house in the evening, he witnessed the lights of the houses coming on one after the other. Various kinds of lights coming on behind big and small windows—a scene he watched many a time from the moving train. Such scenes immediately made him aware of the houses where families were living on rent, the ones where the lights were yellowish, slightly oil-stained and diffident. He used to count them on his way back and arrive at the conclusion that there were more tenants than landlords in this world. Or else the world at night would have been far more luminous every day.

Such was their house too. The only consolation being theirs was visible from aeroplanes. He has never seen it himself, but many a time he has seen the planes up close from the roof during their descent en route to Dum Dum Airport. If any passenger were to look down from the plane window that very instant, they would be able to spot Pushkar's house and tell it was a rented one. That was nothing to be ashamed of, at least not for Pushkar. Many people don't even have a roof over their heads, those who are barely discernible as human beings from planes and trains.

Although, in his own sliver of a room, he hardly switches on the lights most evenings even after it's dark. Not because he is embarrassed or anything. Rather, he is fond of watching the light die out slowly and darkness descend all of a sudden. To wrap that feeling around himself—as if the only reason the day had dawned was to bring him this cover. Thus, many an evening he spends in the darkness of his small, square room. Just above the study table is a light on the oil-stained walls, one that he does not switch on every day. Like he will not today, he thinks.

It's still early afternoon though, he just finished lunch a while back. Baba is on a day shift today, he will be late. Ma is getting some shut-eye, for soon she will have her singing classes in the adjacent room. This is what he is used to since childhood—his father's job as a journalist in the newspaper office and his mother singing at local concerts and teaching music at home. This is how things have been for them, how they still remain. So, the days don't really change for them, they mostly remain the same and Pushkar, too, can predict what will come to pass and when. Like today, like how he was not going to switch on the lights this evening.

Most days, he gets held back in his room, does not get to go out. His first-year classes have just begun. Geography. An excellent subject and it's taught very well at their college. Yet, he is absent more than half the days. It's not that he does not want to go, it's just that he cannot bring himself to do so, always getting stuck. Mornings roll into afternoons and afternoons into evenings; he shuts the shaky doors of his room and sits alone on the far end of his bed, unable to leave. Perhaps because of the windows divided by the rain and snow. He cannot seem to fathom what he needs to do to go out, how he must prepare so he can walk down the narrow lane of their locality towards the main road, where the evening gathers together streams of light that split and disperse all around again.

The far end of his bed is right next to the window, not a single window but a pair of them, almost as if they were twins. In fact, they *were* twins. The same colour, similarly patterned grills, the same prints on the curtains. Were they girls or boys? Pushkar has tried to figure that out for years, ever since they moved into this house. He has not managed to understand it completely, but these days, it seems to him they are surely girls. Boys, brothers, no matter how close they are to each other, they begin to drift apart and become different people as they come of age. They cannot stay side by side, it's something Pushkar has noticed. Sisters, on the other hand, cling to each other and it's nearly impossible to separate them if they are twins. Had they been boys, even these windows would have moved at least a little apart in all these years, but that has not happened. So Pushkar concluded that these two clinging windows at the far end of his bed were, in fact, sisters.

Beyond one of them he can see it rain, beyond the other he finds snow. This has been going on for some time. Previously, it used to happen once or sometimes twice a month. Now it's twice or thrice a week. The scene outside does not alter, it's still the same tiny neighbourhood with its brick-lined road, the same ancient, moss-grown, crumbling walls ending in rusted grill gates beyond which are the same old houses, long-standing members of the area. But the scene appears different through the windows, with the rain and the snow. Sometimes he speculates it's a plot the twin windows have hatched to keep him confined to the room. Yet, neither can he chalk it up to a lie and leave. Most days, he cannot decide whether to go out with an umbrella or to don sweaters and woollens, managing never to leave.

Like today, this moment, as dusk is about to settle, he can clearly see the soft snow outside the window on the left and the torrential rain outside the one on the right. It's been like this since morning and Pushkar knows it will go on like this well past evening until darkness settles like a shroud and obscures everything from sight anyway. He sits quietly on his bed facing the windows, his chin resting on his arms and his gaze fixed outside.

Outside the window on the left, it's been snowing since morning. At first, it was just flakes falling softly, now it's a steady stream. The moss on their overgrown, slimy walls is not visible any more, the bright green appears white. A thick layer of snow has settled on the slender lamp post of the neighbourhood. On the other side is Tarit-babu's house. Minoti's mother had hung clothes to dry on the roof in the morning, but they are frozen solid now. A red kurta, a beige saree, two white pyjamas and a pair of brown trousers—all covered in snow, looking as if they will never move again. Tupul's cat is perched atop Tarit-babu's wall, its already-white fur glistening brighter in the snow. Pushkar can see it has begun to feel the cold, it's curling up further. Looking past the corner of the window, a little further in the distance, one can see the TV repair shop owned by Rontu's family. The shutter is not clearly visible owing to the snow, surely there's a thick layer of it covering their garden already.

Barun's father and Uncle Suhas are returning home together, walking their cycles beside them. In the afternoons,

Puskhar often sees the two of them head to the local library, chatting as they walk back home. Pushkar knows they even play chess together. Their houses stand side by side at the end of the street. From behind his window, he can clearly see the two older friends, brushing the snow off their heads as they walk past the left window and down the lane. As soon as they cross over to the side of the right window, they get drenched in the pouring rain. Neither seems to notice it as they chat and walk—totally soaked, eventually disappearing in the distance, past the window. The window. The frame. Empty screens for scenes to unfold. Two frames on his window, Pushkar thinks. All he has to do is edit it all together.

The courtyard of Poly's house is completely wet, there's no one at home. A mynah sits perched on their ledge, shaking itself dry but not flying away. Maybe it knows it will be worse off in the snow. Two girls walk back in the rain from Shantanu-da's coaching centre—Priyanka and Tuhina; he knows them, knows their names, but they have never spoken. They are all drenched, right from their hair and their clothes to their books. As soon as they walk past a window to the next, they pass into the snow-clad scene. This is all Pushkar has been watching the entire day sitting alone by the windows. No one spares him a glance, it's as if he does not exist. As if the world on his side of the two windows is an entirely alien one. And perhaps it really is, he thinks. That is why he did not leave the house today.

The only thing he has noticed is how the falling rain and snow have gradually begun to resemble spears of light in the darkness. Unbeknown to him, dusk has settled. The slender lamp post with the icy hat casts a modest light. Baba is far away at work, hunched over his table writing features or op-eds on his pad for tomorrow's edition. Is it raining there? Or is there snow? It's all Pushkar can think of. That is his favourite thing to do. To think, in waking or in sleep, thoughts of various kinds. Things that cannot be shared with anyone ever. And yet, he dwells on those thoughts because nothing brings him more comfort than the sheer act of thinking.

The other thing that does bring him reprieve is music. The kind that has just begun to emerge from the adjoining room, like it does every day. Every evening, many people, from near and far, come for music classes with Ma. Most are youngsters, although there a few senior members as well. The strain is struck on the *tanpura*. *Ni Sa Sa Sa*. A pure *nishad*, the seventh note of the octave, as Pushkar can tell. From the darkness of his room, he can even guess which tanpura it is. It's the one he had secretly named Chhutki, the smallish, willowy, maroon one. That's the one playing. *Ni Sa Sa Sa*. '*Sakhi yeri aali piya bin, sakhi kal na padat mohe, ghadi pal chhin din*' [My dearest friend, without my beloved, I feel wretched, as every second feels like a lifetime]. It is Mandira-di who is singing. Such a mature voice! She comes here from Kudghat. '*Sakhi yeri aali*.' Raag Yaman. It's evening in the other room too. Has Mandira-di come in a sweater? Or does she have an umbrella with her? Pushkar really wants to know, but he does not feel like getting off the bed and opening the door to find out. That's how it is most days, he does not feel like leaving this world and venturing into the other.

'*Jabse piya pardes gawan kin . . .*' The higher *Sa*. Chhutki sounds sprightly. She's older than him, no less than an elder sister, a didi, but listening to her it would seem she's just been made. Pushkar can now hear his mother too, showing the others how to sing the last bit, '. . . *gawan kin*'. Mandira-di's *Sa* was not sitting right. It's all in the aim. The aim, the mark, the target. As the thought crosses his mind, he gets up to switch on the light in his little room. He had thought he would not, but he still does. The pale light of a rented house. A narrow bed, a study table on one side reeling under a pile of books, a chair in front of it. That's all Pushkar has. Plus there's one more person: Diego Maradona. A poster bought during the 1990 World Cup still stuck on the door. Even Maradona appears a little washed out in this light. The picture was originally from the 1986 World Cup, from the Germany–Argentina match. The picture was taken as Maradona was passing two players and charging into the D-BOX just before the goal. Shot. Frame. Scene. Speed. Speed that has died down. Astonishing! Only an image can arrest such enormous speed in a frame and hold it in place. It's still someone running, but the moment has been frozen in time, or so it seems to Pushkar.

Today, as soon as the lights come on, he draws the curtains closed, just as the girls pass by. Or else people always glance inside, at least once. He thinks of something, peels himself off the bed and approaches his desk, pausing in front of it for a moment.

'*Jabse piya pardes gawan kin . . .*'

Pardes, a foreign land . . .

Sa.

Aim.

Mark.

Target.

Is it because it's a foreign land that the notes sometimes don't land right? How is one to reach one's goal then? How can one look upon a foreign land from so far away? The road appears blurry in the rain and the snow. Pushkar pauses to think and then opens the cover of his desk to pull out a diary bound in blackish-red rexine. The diary he always wants to keep hidden.

His diary of poems.

2

'Have you read Marcel Proust?'

The silence that greets this question, if divided by two, would be just enough to sublet a small room by the highway at night. Low on rent, the food not too reliable and it usually takes time to fall asleep there.

'I understand. André Gide? Have you?'

The silence that answers this one, with a just a little more added to it, would get you an apple orchard on a hilltop where desolate workers turn up once a week, the wind on the rest of the days, in silence.

'Not even that? Alright. James Joyce?'

This silence is enough to stir envy in a sturdy vase or neatly folded washed curtains in a house that's been locked for ages, a house where no mail arrives any more.

'Goodness! You haven't read Kafka either, have you?'

Now the silence will break, like softly crushed peanut shells.

'Yes, I have. Just *The Metamorphosis*.'

Pushkar's reply is soft. There are at least eight other people in the longish room, all staring at him—the new entrant, small, slim, dishevelled hair and unkempt beard, the boy named Pushkar. Dressed in a kurta and a pair of faded jeans teamed with an equally raggedy *jhola* bag, the boy looks exceptionally innocent and out of sorts, like an unused boat tied at the fisherman's wharf because it cannot withstand the waves of the sea. Or like old magazines folded on benches at a saloon, magazines whose gloss and relevance have long faded, but ones that idle customers do leaf through from time to time. One can also say he resembles the narrow balcony of some cheap hotel where discarded things are dumped throughout the year and where only a few venture once in a while. These are all similes of Pushkar's own invention whenever he stands in front of a mirror. He has no way of knowing if the people staring at him think the same of him.

These questions are not from them but from the boy his age sitting on the bed. Nirban. Surprisingly, this room, too, has two adjacent windows right next to the bed. These just have a sliver of the wall separating them, as in they are not twins. There is a fine, expansive field outside where the colours of a football match have begun to appear in the afternoon. The sun is about to set as it is meant to, there is no rain or snow in sight. Does the world not split outside other people's windows? Is that why people manage to go to college and office on time? As he asks himself these questions, he cannot help but think what on earth had possessed Abhijit to drag him here.

'Do you make anyone read what you write?'

Abhijit asked this question as he grabbed a handful of *moori*, puffed rice, for himself. They were in his house, sitting in the small, dark veranda. This must have been nearly a year back. This was not the earlier, hesitant kind of darkness. This was darkness of a more refined kind, surely because it was Abhijit's own house and not a rented one. It was around the last days of school; after years of being nurtured in the warmth of those uniforms they were about to be released into the world. All grown up, in body and mind. Abhijit was the 'first boy' of the class, Pushkar was never anything like that. Yet they were friends, a friendship that had formed simply on its own. Growing up together, a love for reading, their preferences in music, these things matched so perfectly that it was impossible to not be friends. Besides, they were five boys huddled together in one tiny bench in their classroom. The rest of the room belonged to the boisterous girls, many of whom Pushkar was quite scared of. They were quarrelsome, some were known to pick fights, not letting the boys anywhere close to them. All except one, but more on her later. Nonetheless, the boys stuck together. Consequently, without either of them realizing, Pushkar and Abhijit became friends. Which meant coming back from school, freshening up, changing and then taking an auto to Abhijit's house. A bright stretch of road, a paved lane, an old wavy bridge over the canal, a dimly lit path, a slip of a track and then Abhijit's two-storeyed house. This was the route.

They were sitting and chatting that day on the first-floor veranda when Kakima, Abhijit's mother, came by and placed a large ewer of moori in front of them. As if she firmly supported this conversation but held no expectations whatsoever. Abhijit picked up a handful and asked him the question again.

'Do you make anyone read what you write?'

'Which ones?'

'Obviously I'm not talking about your economics notes here. Your poems. Did you have someone read them?'

'You have read them.'

Pushkar helped himself to some moori although picking out the chillies in the darkness was turning out to be a difficult chore, like stalking a convict through a forest in the dead of night.

'Yes, I have read a few. But someone else has read many more?'

Since this was an uncomfortable question, Pushkar silently thanked the elegant dimness and picked out a nut instead.

'Someone else? Who else?'

'Listen, don't put on that act with me. You make Saheli read all your stuff. She takes your diary home, reads it and then brings it back to you. Everyone knows that.'

As soon as he heard her name, seated right there on the floor of that veranda, the image of a blue border on a plain white saree flashed through Pushkar's mind. As if someone had hung the saree out to dry in faded sunlight and the fabric—the gradually changing and growing school uniform—simply refused to dry out completely. Refusing to shake the scent of dampness off itself. The name of that scent was Saheli too. The name of a wristwatch with a thin, black leather strap. The name of the afternoon sunlight that filtered through the latticed windows of the school corridors. And even the name of the shy tiffin box with the brown lid. And the names of many more things. Saheli. People's names are often not just their own, Pushkar understood this now.

'She took it once to read it. So what?'

Pushkar fielded the defence in the low voice of a novice lawyer, the tone readily betraying that he had lost the round.

'Even that everyone knows. Anyway, let it be. But someone or the other has to read them.'

What Pushkar could not understand was why he had to make someone read the stacks of poems in his diary. Truth be told, except for Saheli and Abhijit no one even knew the diary existed. His parents knew that he would often shut himself in his room and write, but Pushkar had never let them read any of it. He had not let anyone, other than Abhijit and Saheli. What he *had* done was gathered contacts of various journals and sent in his writings to them, but none of them were published yet. Therefore, he was rather reserved about his poetry.

'Why? Why must I have someone read them? I write on my own whim.'

'Don't be stupid. Everyone writes like that. But if you don't make a few other people read them, you will never know how they are. Only Saheli and I can't be your critics. And I'm sure she has nothing but good things to say to you about them.'

Pushkar wanted to avoid that topic for sure, but he also wanted any excuse to hear that name again and again. It felt nice, felt good, it was comforting. Saheli. Again and again. He did not want to talk about her. But he knew this was hardly possible.

'Forget that. Who do I ask to read this? Friends from the neighbourhood? Or do I ask the others in class tomorrow? Does that work? Can you make people read poetry like this?'

The bowl of moori was almost empty. There was a single peanut nestled among the crusty bits, completely out of place as Pushkar could make out in the darkness. No sooner did he notice it than Abhijit picked it up.

'I don't think I'm being able to explain this to you. See, you have a serious outlook regarding poetry. Don't you?'

Pushkar remained quiet. A part of it was because of the last peanut he had missed out on, he knew that. Abhijit went on.

'Let's assume you do. If that is true, then you have to get into some sort of a routine, make it a practice. I'm not asking you to sit down to write every day, like how we go to school. Creative pursuits don't take shape like that. But you must have some sort of a regular exchange, a regular dialogue, vis-à-vis poetry. It cannot just be you writing some poems, making a couple of your friends read it or sending it off to a bunch of places. Rather, I'm talking about a way of life.'

'I get it.'

This was said out of compulsion. Exchange, dialogue— Pushkar was generally afraid of such terms. Every day. Dialogue meant more people, new ones, strangers, incomprehensible. Exchange, too, meant more new people, different ones, distant. It was difficult for him to think of more people in his life. That one room, the twin windows, their tiny locality and the school, perhaps things would have been best if they could have remained the same. That their school life was over was something he did not like thinking about, and that evening as they sat talking, Abhijit suddenly said, 'No, you don't get anything. Come on Sunday. I'll take you to Nirban's. I'll introduce you to him.'

'Nirban? Who's that? And why must I go meet him all of a sudden?'

This time Kakima arrived with two cups of tea, again with the same tacit and unassuming approval. Liquor with sugar, steaming.

'Nirban is a childhood friend of mine. We were in the same school for a while before I took a transfer to our school.'

'But why do I have to go to his house?'

'Listen to the whole thing first. Nirban runs a journal called *Ebong Shomoy*. It's good. He's the editor and there are five or six other people, all writers, his friends. They bring it out about thrice a year, it's done with a lot of love and care. It has their own work, but they also source work from outside. The best part is they meet every week for discussion. They plan the journal, read out their new work to the group and discuss whatever they have been reading. This is important, this sort of an association, to be among other writers. It will be healthy for you. You will receive an honest assessment of your work. Also, it will help create a space for your work in publishing. It will serve as a platform.'

Pushkar fell silent at his words. He was afraid of revealing his poems to so many people at once. As soon as Abhijit finished speaking, he put in a tape in their old cassette player and hit play. 'Gaanwallah.' When the strains of the song rung out in the washed-out, bluish light of that chic, tiny veranda: '*Ei je dekhchi abchhayatai lagche bhalo*' [It seems I have grown fond of the haze], the music, the evening, the fading horns of the rickshaws in the distance, the hazy gatherings on the street corners, the sound of fish being fried in some house in the vicinity, lights coming on in some attic and TVs being switched on, it all began to seem illusory to Pushkar. As if these sights and sounds always existed, everything was going on as usual and yet none of it seemed real. Like Saheli. It was this man's songs that were causing all of this to happen over the past few years. Suman Chattopadhyay. Why did the man need to sing such songs at such a time? When he was about to lose both his head and heart to poetry, his attraction to Saheli, his parents' constant quarrels, why was this man hell-bent on wreaking further havoc on his mind? The man was known for doing this, all the time, this Suman Chattopadhyay.

'Yes, I have. Just *The Metamorphosis.*'

From that evening a year ago, from Suman Chattopadhyay's booming voice and lively guitar and the bowl of moori, Pushkar drags himself back to the present, to Nirban's room, this afternoon. Even after that evening, he had managed to evade this visit for nearly a year, until today when Abhijit succeeded in dragging him to their Sunday gatherings. Now, standing there in front of them, he can see himself on an invisible stand, an accused about to argue his case in front of the jury. These people must be well read; they have surely not spent their entire time staring out of windows.

'That's fine. There's nothing to worry about. Have a seat. You will have tea, right?'

The first half spoken like a doctor, the second like an old friend. He is neither of the two. Pushkar has never been able to lapse into the informal on meeting someone for the first time. With some, he cannot do it even after more than one meeting. Nirban is a lot more self-assured. Behind the thick glasses his eyes seem resolute, as if he knows all that he must do. This resolve seems to dust even his messy curly hair; an able-bodied, bright and fresh-faced youth, not at all like him, Pushkar knows.

The rest of the group comes up to Pushkar and introduce themselves: Soutak, Simanta, Anuja, Anuroop, Khurshid, Manideepa and Saswata. One by one, they come and shake Pushkar's cold, clammy hands. They are writers, they write poetry, stories, essays. They write. Being in the presence of so many writers makes Pushkar want to curl up even more, especially when Nirban asks, 'Is that jhola empty? Or have you brought us some of your work?'

There is a smile on Nirban's face, warm and inviting. He continues, 'Don't be shy. Read out a couple. We all read out our own works here. Get them out, quickly!'

> How much more must it darken
> For you to accept our cloud-grey gaze,
> How many more ups and downs
> For you to believe in life,
> How many more arrows
> For you to know that we have prepared for war,
> Because you know we can never fully forget;
> The flowers drawn on the armour
> And these winding flighty lines that I write
> Will all vanish in the wind.
> Yet, news gathers in this fortress,
> In the bones of our jaws . . .
> No matter how you raise your arms and summon
> We, too, are past whisperers . . . there are many old things
> we know!

Silence.

Just the sound of lips sipping on tea.

The cheering of a game of football from the field nearby.

The sound of evening birds chirping in the trees.

The rest is silence.

As Pushkar puts his diary back inside the jhola, Nirban says, 'Wow, that's beautiful! Has it been published?'

Pushkar shakes his head to say no. Where will his work be published? Who will publish it? Why would they? He has no answers to these questions.

'Then make a fresh copy right away and leave it with me. We will print it. Our next issue comes out next month. What about the rest of you, didn't you like it?'

For Pushkar's bashful ears, this is the moment when the voices of the youngsters around him start to grow dim. Abhijit, having finished his tea, is leafing through a book. He has brought Pushkar here today and affixed him here, like a brick in a new wall or an empty coach behind a speedy engine, and now his work is done. Pushkar draws a full-scape paper to himself and copies the piece carefully. With the care needed for a piece that someone wants to publish after hearing it the first time. With all the attention deserving of something seven or eight people had quietly listened to. He folds the paper and extends it to Nirban, who takes out a rather heavyset book from his bookshelf.

Downstairs, as Pushkar and Abhijit stand waiting at the door, Nirban unfolds the sheet and reads the poem once more. Pushkar's hesitation, a usual feeling whenever someone reads his writing in front of him, seems to disperse with the chittering of insects and the twinkling fireflies.

Nirban says again, 'This is very beautiful. But why doesn't it have a title? What's the name of the poem?'

Pushkar had forgotten all about that.

'The Past Whisperer,' he replies in a low, faint voice.

'Take this. Begin with this book. There's no hurry, read it and return it to me once you're done, alright?'

'Which book is this?' Pushkar asks in surprise.

The sky around them has taken on a shade of orange and purple, a time when Pushkar often feels the blues for no particular reason. Today is different, though.

'Sometimes the past seems farther away than our past life, isn't it? That's when you feel like a past whisperer. Just like your poem. This book is like that too. The testimony of a past whisperer.'

In the dying light, Pushkar looks down and notices a long name written in a beautiful font on the cover of the book.

Remembrance of Things Past.

3

As you step out of Gunjan sir's house, the road winds past the lake straight towards the Selimpur crossing. On this street stands Ma Janani Stores, a shop laden with many things, where a radio plays all the time. At one spot, three *phuchka-wallah*s ply their trade side by side, their tiny lamps flickering like fireflies in the evening. Further down the road is a row of benches where seniors gather to chat in freshly ironed clothes as if on their way to work afterwards. The stretch ends in a glistening market of fresh fish lit by a row of high-powered bulbs while a chain of old rickshaws wait endlessly where it begins. This path, which asks you to get back home quickly but never lets you do so in winter and spring, is not something Asmita *has* to take. Her house is not too far from Gunjan sir's, and she can reach home via any of the smaller alleys there. In fact, that's what she does on most days. Dodging fights erupting in one house, skirting gossip from another or being driven by evening music recitals from some other, is how she reaches their single-storeyed medium-sized house with a grilled veranda. Inside, a bright tube light is on, confident—like the lights of private properties—and her older sister sits studying for her MSc finals next year.

This is how Asmita returns home most evenings, but there are days when she does not. On those days she takes the road by the lake, through the constant cool breeze and the light commotions. It's always a pleasure walking on such roads, and that's exactly how it makes her feel. She would have taken this route every day had it not been for the strict rules at home. And if there wasn't something else stirring up at home, something that she can no longer tolerate. That is why after her first-year classes for the day are over, with the sun setting in the horizon, she does not feel like going back. The reason why on this Saturday evening she is reluctant to get back home after Gunjan sir's tuition classes, and why even if she does get back, all she wishes to do is lock herself up in her room and be alone. Not exactly alone, with Kufri actually. Their pet Labrador Retriever, Kufri, except who, Asmita knows, no one else understands her.

Nevertheless, there is one shining beacon to these Saturday evenings, irrespective of the many other sorrows, and that has to do with Gunjan sir. Back in school, Asmita had three tuition classes, even in college she has two. She sees her other friends attend a variety of them, but she has yet to come across a teacher and human being quite like Gunjan sir. Neither has anyone else she knows of. A professor in the college where Asmita is a first-year student of English literature, he takes tuitions at his house once a week. She has scarcely seen anyone teach like him. For Gunjan sir, there are two worlds: the world of English literature and the real life outside that, even though he keeps judging, or tries to judge, the latter based on the former. Tall and lanky with salt-and-pepper hair and bifocal glasses, always in a pair of brown trousers and a white shirt with the sleeves rolled up, twirling his thin moustache in excitement while teaching or lighting up one cigarette after another, Asmita has often seen this man lose his train of thought while talking. He could be teaching a poem one moment, only to suddenly go quiet and stare fixedly out the window as if someone had yelled 'Statue!' or as if someone had just conveyed some bad news. Outside his window, the evenings are dark, the white glare of the lamp post falls on the water as if trying to avoid catching a cold, and that's when he goes silent.

Then he would begin to talk about his life, going further and further away from the poem he was teaching. And the incredible manner in which he spoke, so surprising the form of his delivery and such a different way of looking at life, that his students would all find themselves immersed in the telling. However, gradually, he would trace the threads of the story right back to the poem they had abandoned. It would seem like magic, and everyone would wonder how the man could weave the impossible so effortlessly with the threads of time. Most days he would ask his students not to write anything down, to take no class notes but try and remember the discussion, to understand it. Writing things down meant not retaining them. Sometimes Asmita would pack up her notebook and listen in rapt attention, trying to retain everything Gunjan sir was teaching. It is much later that she realized one did not need to expend much effort. One only had to listen to Gunjan sir speak in order to remember what was being taught.

So, it seems to Asmita the man lives his life by way of literature, or he thinks of his own life as literature, or perhaps a bit of both. Some days, he would not even cover the syllabus. Instead, he would read them some other text, discuss it or even start an argument over it, or tell them about some author they were never going to read in their syllabus. All in all, Asmita knew every Saturday that tiny flat by the lake with the even tinier room will be able to lift her mood.

There are a few students who Gunjan sir understands better than the others. He is more concerned about them, regards them differently even. Asmita is aware that she is one among them. There are three more years to his retirement. He was married once, or so they say, but now he lives alone. He has a daughter, quite young, who is in school, but not in Kolkata. All of this is hearsay, things the girls discuss. However, despite all these years of teaching, he possesses a novel outlook that makes him fall in love with literature every single day and regardless of the number of students, he feels compelled to provide them individual care and attention. Such things make him worthy of emulation. As she walks by the lake clutching her bag to her chest, these thoughts flicker through her mind.

Perhaps because she is a little more lost in thought than other days, she fails to notice the glare of a bike's headlight, ignores the stone chip that comes and hits her sandals. While she is aware of things around her, her heart really isn't 'watching'. It was Gunjan sir who had drawn her attention to it today. 'I will not ask why you are upset, but you do have to get better.'

As soon as the words hit her, almost unconsciously, tears gathered at the corner of her eye, threatening to spill over.

What a strange trick this was! Her ears were signalling her eyes which were ready to push tears down her cheek. At times it seemed to her as if despair was genuinely fond of the merry-go-round. Today, she did not let the tears roll down her soft cheeks. She stood there, gaze tilted, hands frozen on the brown paper-covered long notebook she had been trying to put inside her bag. Her narrow fishtail braid, almost impossible to tame, fell past her back. Her fair, slender fingers trembled as this petite young girl with a quiet, intelligent face seemed ready to fall apart over one single sentence from her teacher but could not bring herself to do it.

'Sit.'

Gunjan sir came forward and pulled out a chair for her. It dawned on her that there was a sense of relief in getting caught like this. Her parents had never extended a seat to her like this, nor could they ever read what was on her mind. But this man had done it—Gunjan sir. How great it would have been if her father was like this, or if her mother understood her! The thought crossed her mind as she sat on the chair, lightly, as if still floating, still hesitant and sad. Gunjan sir went and stood by the window of the empty room. The window near the light of the brave lamp post. He lit a cigarette, probably his fifth of the evening, and said, 'Happy families are all alike; every unhappy family is unhappy in its own way.' Do you know whose line this is?'

Without looking up, Asmita just shook her head, twice. She sniffled. Her eyes were about to well over; she didn't let them, but she couldn't help a tiny cry. Still staring outside, Gunjan sir spoke, 'You will read it, you must. Tolstoy. Leo Tolstoy's famous words from the beginning of *Anna Karenina*, the first line of the novel, in fact. The novel itself is gigantic like a boat, so it's not easy to compose a line like this right at the outset. The entire novel can be visualized in this line, like watching the expanse of space through a telescope. Asmita, sometimes I feel Tolstoy should not have written the novel. Just this one single line could have been the novel, the rest is just an elaboration of this very idea. Perhaps the rest was written out of greed for this expansion. See how I am digressing yet again?'

His cigarette was burning, and in the air outside coils of smoke like white hair were slowly dissipating. The smell only reached her wet nose when she could finally raise her ashen face.

'The thing is, there's no special achievement in being happy. Not that I'm saying there's some kind of greatness in living a sad life. I am not one to glorify sorrow. What I want to tell you is that a person who can feel sadness must know their heart is their greatest wealth. It is sorrow that sets us apart from each other, makes us unique. Like what Tolstoy says. It is difficult to pick between happy faces placed side by side, but look at ten sad faces, one after the other, and you will be able to tell them apart. Because sorrow makes one different, makes one stand out. At the same time, not everyone can be its host, not everyone can let it find a place in their heart, for grief requires a lot of space. If your heart is not as big as a house, then grief will probably not even be able to get past the door. Isn't that so? Hmm?'

He paused for a moment. As he took two final drags from his cigarette, his eyes closed in pleasure, relief and perhaps a bit of grief as well. She briefly looked up to glance at him. He was standing near her, but in reality, he was much further away—too far away for anyone to reach him.

'You have that kind of a heart. That's why you get hurt, why you feel low. And this is how it will be for the rest of your life. I will not lie to you and say that things will get better. One source of despair gives way to another, like a tourist. Imagine they come to you on vacation: for them, you are a place to put up in for a few days. Your heart is their room of choice, a room from which they can watch the mountains or the valleys. Not everyone's heart is like that. Do we go and visit every city? Just like that, grief does not invade all hearts. They come to you perhaps because the view they find in you is magnificent, try and see if you can find that too. Talk to your feelings, get to know your pain. You're young now, this is the right time. The older you get, the more difficult it will be to get to know someone new, the urge to have a conversation will decline, even with yourself. You're young, talk now, talk to yourself.'

Asmita sensed her eyes failing to hold back tears. They were incredibly strong. Her cheeks were wet before she could finish the thought. Tiny wet lines began to form on them as if furrows had been dug to water the land. Despite her lowered eyes, she could sense Gunjan sir, having finished his cigarette, looking at her fixedly, his gaze unruffled.

'Can you eat food cooked without salt?'

Despite the surprising nature of the sudden question, Asmita remained quiet. Her eyes were so heavy that even shaking her head felt difficult.

'Fish curry, cauliflower curry, moong dal, can you eat any of these without salt? Or for that matter, the phuchkas that you people eat beside the lake after your tuition classes, would you be able to eat it without salt?'

Aware that he was still looking her, she shook her head softly to say no.

'You won't be able to. Because without salt everything seems bland. Grief is a bit like that salt. You're sad because it's there, but without it, life will be left entirely devoid of taste. Such a life would never suit you, would it, Asmita? So, take comfort in the fact that you can feel sorrow. This is not a luxury, neither is this a kind of helplessness. It's just grief, like salt, you don't require much, but you do require it. Perhaps that is why tears are salty too. Like the ones I notice trickling down your face right now.'

He took a white handkerchief out of his pocket and handed it to her. It appeared blurry to her, as did his hands. While racing out of his flat the walls appeared hazy as well, like the out-of-focus flight of stairs that took her outside, leaving her by the lake in the evening. Crowds have a distinct advantage; people can easily vanish in them. Like this slender, fair, shadowy girl quietly walking alone, trying to cross from one side of the lake to the other.

Her old school friends are still her friends. She misses them all the time even when she is in college. Surely they miss her too. Even though the number of these friends was never high in school, they are still there. Pushkar is in her college too, in geography. But the two of them do not get to see each other every day. Neither does she wish to, because meeting him means talking about another one of their friends and Asmita would have to stay quiet on that subject. The friend who was a little more than just a friend, who still is more than just a friend, who is waiting for her today on the other side of the lake in front of the new café. The person whose mention she so desperately wants to avoid that she does not meet Pushkar despite being in the same college. He is waiting for her today, for them to meet. On other days they usually order coffee and sandwiches, but today Asmita feels no hunger or thirst. Gunjan sir's words have shaken her so much that all she wants to do is get back home at the earliest and crawl into bed.

Only today, she must meet him and tell him they can no longer continue to see each other. Her wedding has been fixed and all arguments and uproar regarding it have failed. In front of her parents, immovable like two statues, none of her reasons have borne any fruit. Even their favourite daughter, her older sister, has not managed to do anything. The wedding is to happen by the end of the year, both families are trying to fix a date. She must tell him all about it today. Just like how two years ago, at an empty bus-stop on a rain-heavy Class XI morning, Asmita had confessed her love to him.

As she wipes her tears with Gunjan sir's handkerchief, Asmita notices him. Abhijit, still a little far off, the tiny red-and-blue lights of the café forming a pattern on his shirt, a jhola slung over his shoulders, waiting. A smile still hangs on his lips, a trace of this evening.

4

'Do you know, just because you are here, I can come and tell you everything that's on my mind. If you had not been there, I would never have known that I had so much to say, that even I wanted to talk to someone. If we had never met, I would have never known that. I have never been to a church, but I have heard all churches have a confessional. Do you know that? As in, do you know what that is? A small box within which a priest sits and there's a curtain drawn over it. From the other side of the curtain anyone can come and confess their crimes, their sins. It's meant to ease one's burden, to make one feel lighter. From the other side, the priest advises a way to seek mercy, to turn over a new leaf. I don't go to a church, I come to you instead. You are my only confessional. There are no curtains here, neither are they required. That you can hear me is in itself a huge deal. And I can comprehend your responses too, which is why I keep coming back. Only those who have committed a crime, who have done something wrong, is it only those people who need to confess? Tell me. Those who love, they need it too, don't they? Those who write poetry or sing songs or dabble in theatre, even those who survive without any of these things, they need it too. Don't they? For me, that is how you are. See how I come here from so far? Often these autos refuse to come, and I have to take multiple autos and it costs more, it's inconvenient. But I still come here. The schooldays were best, you were just two stops away and I could walk over if I wanted to. I could make up some story at home to explain why it takes me so much time to get back from school. Not that anyone really asked. Most evenings, Baba was at work and Ma in her music class, leaving me to get back home, lock myself in and lie down in bed. I used to think. One can't be sure what I used to think about exactly . . . just whimsical things. Even now I think every day, though I'm still not sure about what. But do you know, I love it? I believe I would want nothing else if I am allowed to just think. If it were a real job, I would be the first to get it. The only problem then would be that I would have to think on someone else's command. Now I am free to think whatever I want. As I was saying, I would talk to you, get back home and lie in bed, on some days with my hand resting on my diary of poems. I would think back on our conversation that particular afternoon, only to be suddenly reminded of something I had forgotten to tell you that day. The next day, I would visit you again just to tell you what I had missed. Now my college is on the opposite route and that's a problem. It takes me so long to come here that I hardly get to catch a glimpse of you in the bright sunlight. And yet I come, and I will continue to turn up. Do you know why? Because I believe everyone needs a confessional, at least one, their entire life. Its nature might change over time, but it needs to be there. Or else it is impossible to carry all these thoughts around, one would get no work done. When it all seems too heavy, when there are too many things that need to be said, it gives me comfort knowing you are here. That I can come visit you whenever I want to and tell you whatever is on my mind. That you will be okay with it. And so, I come here even if it gets late, even if it's past evening. Oh! See what I have done! I have only been talking about myself. How are you? Are you well?'

A breeze blows in from the direction of Sarovar, perhaps it's best to call it a wind.

A light is switched on at the door of the library in the distance, a group of fresh-faced youngsters step out on the road talking loudly.

A phuchka-seller brings down the red fabric covered basket off his head and settles it on a tripod.

The sound of the shutters of the medicine shop going up in the next lane rings out for a considerably long time.

Someone goes by on a cycle, a radio tied to the handle where a song from *Saajan* can be heard. '*Mera dil bhi kitna pagal hai . . .*' [How crazy my heart is . . .].

The gulmohar tree on the other side of the road suddenly seems to power down, flowers included.

'I get it. This is not a time when you are well. What I have never understood is how someone like you can stand to live here on this busy main road, with all the chaos and the crowd. Does it not become difficult to concentrate? I could have never lived amidst so much colour, so many lights and conversations, so many people coming and going all the time. But do you know, let me tell you, I don't think I could have lived without it either. Does it seem to you that I'm talking nonsense? Let me explain. I write poetry, you know that. Perhaps it amounts to nothing. My poems keep getting turned down by magazines and journals all the time, but that doesn't stop me from writing because I love it. I do it in hiding. Not everyone knows about it, just a handful, including you. But how do I write? As much as I write at home, on my bed or sitting at my desk, I also write as I roam around. It's been a while since I have managed to do that, I have told you why. Those two windows are to blame. But the days I do manage to go out, I roam around in many places. It was something I could never do earlier; it was weird walking around in a school uniform. And they used to scold me a little at home too. Now I can do it. I walk out of college and keep walking till I reach the Nandan quadrangle or the crossing of Lindsey Street, some days I take a more circuitous route and walk till the Park Circus crossing. One day, I even went as far as Shyambazar. Everything is new that side of town, but the crowd I can recognize pretty well. What do I do there? I look for poetry. The words that keep turning in my head, those that want to take form on paper, I sit with them somewhere. Park benches, roadside tea stalls, the lobby outside ticket counters, long porticos of house, even the hard iron chairs at bus stops. I sit down and take out pads of paper. Newsprint—Baba brings back a lot of it from office, some of which I take before leaving the house. Paper and pens. You might not believe me, but when I sit down with pen and paper, the moment the pen touches the surface of the sheet, a curtain drops around me. A separation, sort of like a confessional. I can clearly sense it; I may not be able to explain it to you properly, but it's there. In an instant it shields me from everything going on around me, as if I'm present but not really *there*. As if I can observe everyone, but no one can catch a glimpse of me. I don't know how this magic happens, perhaps it is the same with everyone who touches pen to paper. When that happens, I begin to write, words come to me as if in a daze. I know I ought to be more careful when I write, be more meticulous, but I cannot seem to avoid the daze. Why am I telling you all this? Well, a few days ago, we had gone on a five-day trip to Himachal. It was not a vacation, it was a college excursion. I have never been to such a beautiful place. I have never been anywhere, really. We were put up in a dormitory, one simply had to open the window to get a view of the mountains and the clouds. There were no people, no commotion, nothing. I thought I could finish many a poem, but I could not even manage to write one. That's when I understood that solitude is entirely a relative thing, silence too. I cannot understand myself without the immense tumult of this city, that's where my silence lies. Unless I am standing in this swiftly moving crowd, I cannot find any solitude. The silence of nature sounded odd to my ears that day, the seclusion constantly battered me, making it difficult for me to write. You know what, there must be this sense of magic. The curtains need to come down as soon as pen touches paper.'

At the third-floor window of the house up ahead, a young girl parts the curtains and peeks out. Perhaps she's about to sit down to study or she's waiting for someone.

A dosa seller walks past with his square wooden cart striking a tone on the hot *tawa* with his metal tongs.

There is a temple somewhere nearby, the sound of bells ringing fills the air.

Someone is burning dry leaves, there's smoke all around.

A couple passes by holding hands, immersed in a bashful conversation.

The cat that had been trying for long to jump from the wall of one house to another finally succeeds.

'Can I tell you something? Only if you don't mind. Yes, I can stay awhile. I may not wear a watch, but that's probably why I have a good sense of time. It's around six-thirty now, isn't it? Then we have time. These days, nobody says anything even if I return as late as eight in the evening. Have you ever seen poems that have been turned down? Perhaps not since you don't write. Those who write have seen them, at least I have. I see such poems from time to time. I send them far and wide, carefully folded in pristine white envelopes, neatly sealed with glue and a properly placed postage stamp on top. I send them far, to various journals and newspapers. Renowned places where many people are published. I used to dream, do you know, that one day my work, too, will be in such publications. Little magazines. The very term used to send a shiver down my spine. There are so many of them and they have such exquisite editions. The long list of contents comprises numerous poets, their astounding works gracing the pages within. I used to wonder if my work, too, will be published in such places. And so I send my poems to them. However, most of them are returned to me. Those who do not wish to hurt me usually write a softly worded note of rejection. Those who do not have the time for such considerations simply send a postcard saying they cannot publish my poem because it has not been selected. Some don't even bother to do that; one just has to assume that it did not work out. Nowadays it has become a routine for me, receiving such rejections. Previously, I used to get very upset. I used to think: why can't they take a chance and publish it? Now I don't think like that. I try to understand why it wasn't selected. Maybe because it couldn't become a poem, wasn't a good enough piece of writing. I sit with them again, to reflect, to figure out how to make them better. There's no one to teach me, no one I can talk to about such things. So, I come to you, to tell you everything. You are my confession box. There's a certain joy in being turned down, you see. There's a certain pleasure in rejection. For that, one does not need to think of oneself as superior or inferior. All one needs to do is soak in the feeling. Now I have grown to like it, to like all kinds of rejection. And yet, when I glance at my poems that have been sent back, I experience this odd sensation. As if I had sent them to complete a task which they couldn't, or I had sent them off to fight a war which they lost. Or I had sent them to the store to shop on credit and they have come back insulted. The poems remain quiet while I try and explain to them why this coming back is important. I resolve to send them again, to distant places, to chart their own paths. At times I think even if none of my poems get published, not in any magazine or journal ever, that doesn't mean my efforts are not sincere. Why do I write? Because I cannot exist without it;

not writing suffocates me, that's why. Why should I connect that with the work getting published? Just because they are mine, does it also make it my burden to ensure they reach everyone? So nowadays I explain these things to my writings, I chat with them and try to put them back together. My room is now full of these rejected poems, and I spend my time with them. There's another thing I must tell you. I have made a few new friends. They run a magazine and want to publish one of my poems. I should agree, right? What do you think?'

On the main road up ahead, a bus has nicked a car. There's a crowd, a fight is about to break out.

The cement mixture running in the nearby construction site falls silent.

A plane flies past overhead, its lights blinking like a red firefly.

A rally is on the move somewhere. Their slogans are audible over the loudspeaker, but their demands aren't exactly clear.

The jingling sounds of anklets along with that of a tabla drift in from some house nearby. Must be a music class going on.

Another draught blows in from the direction of the Sarovar lake, this one ought to be called a wind too.

Pushkar stops for a moment. To catch his breath. In his head, where he had been talking. The monologue was tiring him, so he pauses for a bit. The soul has a language too—it can speak, it can feel under pressure as well. Especially after a long, continuous conversation. But he has no choice. He can come here for an hour to an hour and a half, at most. If he cannot say whatever is in his heart in that time, then it will be futile to go back home and sit with a geography textbook. He will not be able to put his mind to it. Without finishing the conversation, he knows his soul will keep pacing, it will not rest anywhere for a moment.

He is standing on the sidewalk of a wide road somewhere between Southern Avenue and Purna Das Road. On one side, the tall fence of Ravindra Sarovar is visible, and on the other, there's traffic on Purna Das Road. This is his favourite street. There are many thoroughfares in Kolkata that he likes, where he has taken strolls, but none of them are like this road. For his long-time confession box lives on this road, his closest friend who knows all his secrets till date. A milkwood tree.

In early autumn, when the tree is in full bloom, he does not come and talk so much. The fragrance, then, is so intoxicating that he ends up standing still beneath the tree like a man possessed. But during the rest of the year, he comes and has long conversations with the tree. The tree never replies, just listens to everything that Pushkar has to say. And Pushkar knows it understands him. When the wind blows and the branches and leaves shiver, it becomes clear the tree is listening to him, listening to his every word.

It's time now to get back. To get into the long queue for autos or take multiple autos or somehow throw oneself at the mercy of a crowded bus. But today he will be going back unburdened, so none of that worries him. Once a weight has been lifted off the heart, the body seems lighter too, Pushkar has noticed. It is past seven now, he has to get back. In the dim shadows of the road, he glances up at his confession box once more—steadfast, with a thick trunk and densely coiled canopy, this old milkwood tree.

He walks closer to the tree.

Places his palm on its thick coarse bark.

Before anyone notices he quickly hugs the base of the trunk for a moment.

This is the tree in which all his words are saved, in which his life resides.

'I'll be off today. And I almost forgot to tell you. I am in love with Saheli. Completely.'

5

'Latt uljhi suljha ja balam, latt uljhi suljha ja . . .'
[My hair has gone astray, beloved, help me set it right . . .]

Again and again, Pritha finishes the *sargam* and returns to the *mukhda* of the fast Teen Taal Bandish. She returns very well, just as a deft shepherd returns after a day of herding cattle or a tram retires to its depot after a whole day of commute. But the fact that she can infuse her return with something a little more exquisite makes it a song, a tune, a *raag*, a *bandish*. And the tiny room of the rented house adorned with the pale lighting and cracked red floors fills to the brim with that exquisiteness. Girls of various ages are seated on an old bluish rug that is so frayed that the threads have scattered all over the place. They have their knees tucked together so that there is space for everyone, so that all of them can happily fit into this tiny room. They, too, come from such small and dimly lit houses, some from the neighbourhood, some from afar, to take singing lessons every evening. It's an attachment for them, it's also freedom.

Her eyes closed, Pritha continues to sing. She has recently started teaching psychology in a college. Her father passed away six months ago from cancer, he never got to know about his daughter's new job. Her mother, too, had passed a long time ago and Pritha now lives in a two-room house, on rent like this one, with her brother and sister-in-law. Ever since her father died Pritha has been miserable. Try as she might, she cannot bring herself to enjoy her new job. Only when she turns her mind to music, when she closes her eyes, moves aside the veil and immerses herself in its depths, that everything in the world around her seems to simply vanish. When her fingers brush against the strings of the tanpura, everything else ceases to exist and she finds herself slipping past all the gloom into a different world—the world of music.

Ishita has a lot of faith in this student of hers. Irrespective of poverty, grief and job-related issues, she has a real gift for music. The kind of gift that cannot be driven away either. If any of the other girls makes a few mistakes here and there, Ishita immediately stops them, scolds them and corrects them. But the fact that she never stops Pritha at all is something the others have noticed. Ishita never stops her simply because she can sense true musical talent in Pritha. Take Bihag, for instance. Such a wonderful evening raag. Just as it comprises the tremors of sensuality and the fulfilment of submission, it also encompasses the agony of separation. It is not easy to sing a raag that is produced from a confluence of so many things. Pritha can do it, Ishita can see it right in front of her. It's not that Pritha can see it, rather she can visualize the music flowing from within her. Without being able to visualize in such a manner, one cannot really listen to music and Ishita firmly believes this. '*Latt uljhi suljha ja balam . . . Mathe ki bindiya bikhar gayi hai, apne haath sajaa jaa baalam . . .*' Tears softly roll down Pritha's cheeks, but Ishita does not stop them. When music and tears mix somewhere, they should not be stopped and Ishita knows this very well.

Ishita—she with the shoulder-length hair; the thick, high-powered glasses; lips stained with a tint of strong *zarda* and paan; and a voice that can reach any point of a composition—is someone everyone regards with the utmost respect. Not just her students, even connoisseurs of music, at the mere mention of her name, instantly recall some of her memorable musical performances. A soft-spoken but strong-willed woman. Ishita's father, too, was a singer. Her training began while accompanying him on stage shows when she was just four years old. It has been many years since her father's passing. It has also been many years since she fell in love with a music-crazy journalist, married him and moved into this house in the suburbs. She has an elder brother, who, too, is a well-known singer. The siblings have managed to keep the last embers of their family's musical legacy alive; neither knows what will happen after they are gone.

There's another reason why Ishita commands such respect and that has to do with her steadfast spirit. Earlier, music was appreciated solely on its merit in this country and that is what Ishita has grown up knowing. But now things are changing. Public relations—the term represents a union of ideas, but it only serves to cause more disruption. She can sense it. Considering the number of places in the country and abroad she has received invitations from and the people she has sung for day and night, their situation ought to have been a lot different. She should not have needed to take to eight-hour classes every day of the week. By now she should have been known by more people, should have been closer to fame, instead of shunning awards she should have easily won. But it is against her nature to bow down to anything other than music. Not just that, Ishita is determinedly forthright when it comes to things she does not like. She can sense that offers for shows are dwindling and calls from organizers are fast drying up. But she does not dwell on these things. All these students who come to her from far and wide, who surround her, her music and her tiny music room, Ishita is uninterested in pursuing any form of gratification greater than this.

As Pritha reaches the second stanza, Ishita raises her hand, gesturing to her to stop. Her moist eyes had already opened for a moment or someone would have had to physically stir her awake from the thrall of the composition. Noticing Ishita's gesture—her palm spread out as if in blessing, Pritha's singing comes to a stop, her hands pausing on the tanpura. The heartbeat of a house of music is the sound of the tanpura. The tunes that flow from this four- or six-string instrument are the lifeblood that flows through the veins of the house. So, when a tanpura falls silent after a long stretch, everything in the world seems to come to a grinding halt.

Sumit-babu is at the door. Sumit Dastidar, the eastern zonal head of the most renowned recording company. A six-foot-tall, heavy-set, deep-voiced man with a thick moustache, dense hair and bushy eyebrows, at whose office one has to queue up at least a month in advance to lobby for a meeting. A man whose likes and dislikes determine the very fate of musicians and singers as for many of them, even a single record with his company can turn the wheel of fortune in their favour. To date, Ishita does not have a single record or cassette of her songs, neither with Mr Dastidar's company nor with anyone else's. She has never been able to take her music to the people, she is just not that sort of a person. Neither has anyone ever come to her for her music, until today, until Mr Dastidar.

'Oh, Sumit-da, it's you. Please come in, have a seat. Girls, make some space.'

Seated on the floor, her comments are first directed at him and then the girls. Mr Dastidar takes a seat on the small sofa in the corner of the room. Ishita folds her hands in greeting, a smile on her lips, fearless. Rather, it's his answering smile that comes across as a little self-conscious. Pritha gently sets the tanpura on the floor. Sarama and Indrani get up and glance at Ishita, seeking permission. Then one of them turns to go inside to prepare tea in the dingy kitchen, while the other steps out of the house to go buy some sweets and samosas from the nearby Anadi Sweet Shop. No one needs to give them instructions. Ishita's guest is their guest too, they all know it's as much their responsibility to welcome them as it is hers.

'What about this sudden visit? Did you have some work this side of town?' Ishita enquires in surprise, her astonishment totally guileless.

'Not at all. I have come to see you. I did not know your address, but Mr Mukherjee, who was here a long time ago, gave me directions.'

'Really? You could have simply called me.'

'That's okay. I wanted to come see you.'

'Please have some tea first. Thank you, Sarama.'

Mr Dastidar picks up the cup of tea placed in front of him in his broad hands. A tea set bought at a Bengali New Year sale comprising six pieces, of which only two have escaped destruction. A bouquet of roses on white. For him, having tea means pouring the hot beverage on to the saucer and then taking a sip with a satisfied slurp. After a couple of sips, he continues, 'I did call you but could not get through.'

Ishita remembers there has been work going on with the telephone lines of the locality over the past few days.

'Oh yes, the line is out of order. Anyway, at least it got you to come to our house. It's not ours exactly though, we're tenants.'

'Ownership is not always determined by money, hope you know that,' Mr Dastidar replies with a smile before loudly slurping his tea again.

The samosas and sweets arrive.

'Sugar, you know, blood sugar,' he says as he picks up a samosa. The room is silent, no tanpura, no conversation, just speculation. Conjecture from Ishita's end. There is curiosity as well, on the part of the students.

'I have some pressing matter to discuss with you. That's why I'm here.'

Mr Dastidar finishes the samosa and shakes his hand to brush off the crumbs. The fine yellow specks that fall off form a fleeting, decidedly lower middle-class design on the ancient dark red floors.

'Of course, tell me, what is it?' Ishita replies with a kind of detached interest.

'Here? Can we go inside?'

'There's only one room inside, Sumit-da—our bedroom. You can talk here, it's not a problem. I consider them like my children. There is hardly anything I hide from them. We can talk here.'

Mr Dastidar takes a moment to prepare himself and then continues, 'We were thinking of bringing out a cassette of yours. Every year, during Pujo, we bring out a bunch of new releases. This year, we suggested your name at the board meeting. It was my idea. You have been in the music world for so long but not had a single recording. That's not right. So, everyone agreed, it's a unanimous decision. This Durga Pujo, we are recording a cassette with you.'

The silence that greets this declaration is a lot different than the silences we have come across before. In place of curiosity a spark of joy flashes across the faces of the students, in place of anticipation a quiet look of weary satisfaction passes over Ishita's. This is how she has always wanted things. Things she rightfully deserves being offered to her. Not opportunities born of appeals.

'This is delightful, Sumit-da, that all of you have thought of me. But there isn't much time left for Pujo.'

'So what? You won't need special preparations. You have always been involved in music. Plus you know very well we don't record in rented studios. We have a well-equipped set-up of our own. We can fix a date; you just turn up with the instruments you need. Let us know whom you would prefer on the tabla. It's best if you have a couple of options. Forty minutes per side. Your *gharana* is known for the long *khayal*s. So perhaps two long khayals, and it'll be nice if there's a *thumri*. And you are famous for your renditions of the raag Desh. What was that thumri again?'

'*Nadiya bairi bhayi*' [The river has turned against me], Pritha chimes in with a smile on her face, having controlled her excitement. Her eyes are still moist, this time from happiness. Mr Dastidar smiles too.

'Yes, yes. *Nadiya bairi bhayi*. Keep that in the list.'

A slight smile appears on Ishita's face as she replies. 'Fine, Sumit-da. Please leave your number with me. Once the phone is fixed, I will give you a call and plan accordingly.'

Mr Dastidar takes out a visiting card from the pocket of his beige safari suit and hands it to her. As Pritha takes it from him, he says, 'Here you go. But there's one more thing.'

'Yes, tell me what it is.'

Mr Dastidar clears his throat and glances at her. 'You do have to come in for an audition, though.'

The silence that greets this statement is so different from both the previous occasions that it becomes apparent in an instant. It does not last long, though. Ishita breaks the stillness and asks, 'I didn't quite get you, Sumit-da. What do you mean by an audition?'

Mr Dastidar clears his throat again, rather loudly this time, and answers, 'It's nothing, really. A mere formality. I will arrange everything; it will barely take an hour. You have to come and sing something of your choice. The rest you leave to me. I hope you understand, ours is a huge company, we are answerable to the head office. These Bombay people, your name is still a little new to them. Television has totally changed the landscape. For regular artists, things are different. You, as in, you get what—'

Ishita suddenly breaks into a smile. First, staring at the floor, and then, looking directly at Mr Dastidar. Then she says softly, 'I understand, Sumit-da. The fact that even in the midst of all this you have thought of me is a gift in itself. But I don't think you understand, you can't ask me to audition.'

Mr Dastidar falls quiet. He knows Ishita has more to say and he must listen.

'The thing is, I have never asked anyone for anything. Never. But I have definitely given. I have given forty years of my life to music. If I live longer, I will give more. But at this age, after being a musician for so long, I will not audition, Sumit-da. The few listeners I have, I am happy with them. And these students here are my children. What else do I need? I will not audition.'

If it were someone else, Mr Dastidar would have a few more things to say, but he knows Ishita well, the daughter of Guru Ramanath Chakraborty. A gharana of inflexibility just as it is a gharana of long khayals, their no meant a no. He knows there is no point stretching the conversation further, so he gets up to leave. Ishita gently places her hand on Pritha's shoulder and says, 'This girl sings well. Pritha. You must have heard her singing when you were at the door. Ask her to audition. Now, if it's possible. I have been training her myself. Ask her before it's too late.'

Despite his height, Mr Dastidar looks small, his head hanging low. He turns to leave, his face red and grim. Just as he is about to step out of the house, Ishita calls him from behind. Mr Dastidar turns around to find Pritha, holding out the visiting card he had given her earlier.

'Take your card, Sumit-da. Give it to the right person. Don't waste it here. Our phone will never be fixed.'

As he walks out into the dark, tiny sliver of a garden in front of the house, Mr Dastidar hears the tanpura come alive again. Like something that had died for a while coming back to life. '*Latt uljhi suljha ja balam.*' Bihag. Not Ishita's voice. It's the other girl, he thinks to himself stepping into the car.

Pritha.

But just as potent.

And stubborn.

6

'You don't know where to place the accents and here you are trying to type in French. My compositor got annoyed and left in the afternoon. Now it is me who has to type this. If that's what you want, why don't you bring out the whole thing in French? Why be extra smart and use French words in a Bengali text? Every word has three accents, which you are constantly shifting around ten times. Shift one more accent and you will have to find another press.'

Pradip-da lets loose this volley of words as he tries to shift accents around by beating down on the off-white keyboard with loud clicks. Pushkar is meeting him for the first time although Nirban and his friends have known him for a while. For it's at Pradip-da's tiny press that *Ebong Shomoy* has been published for the past three years and in whose next edition Pushkar's poem will be included. Pradip-da is a small, thin man of around fifty. A pair of square frame glasses with strings tied to the temples rests on his nose and a moustache resembling a coconut husk

broom makes his face look all the more serious. Pradip-da
has the manuscripts heaped over his table where he is in
the process of painstakingly singling out recently corrected
accents and then editing them on the computer screen.
The matter must be released at the earliest for it to go for
printing and then binding, hence the hurry.

Pushkar has never seen print matter being composed; he
is not aware of the rules or how the written words are first
transferred from paper to light and then printed out as proofs.
He has never seen a copy meant to be proofread. He has heard
about them from Baba, who always brings proof copies home
while working on the Pujo special edition of his newspaper,
but no one is allowed to touch those. So, for the very first time
Pushkar sees how, despite Pradip-da's immense annoyance,
letters appear on the computer screen. Writings. Words.
Language. Letters. Manuscript. Being arranged in layers, one
by one, like an idol of a god being fashioned from a straw
framework. It is all very fascinating to him, so fascinating that
even Pradip-da's scolding is not enough to strike fear in him.
Pushkar throws a glance at Nirban; he does not appear to be
perturbed either. Rather, he smiles and says, 'Don't worry,
Pradip-da. This one's done. For the next five years, we will not
even consider another issue on French literature.'

'If you do, you won't have Pradip-da's press to print
it,' he replies. 'Just because accents are free, he's put them
everywhere. Why can't these issues be on Manik, Bibhuti or
Tarashankar?

'This boy is a newcomer, Pradip-da. We are including his
poem this time. His name is Pushkar. Are you done composing?
Then please show it to him once so he can take a look.'

Pradip-da turns and looks at him past his square glasses with a severe expression and then declares, 'Let me handle the accents first, then we'll see.'

It was early in the afternoon when Pushkar reached Nirban's house, straight from college. Though not a Sunday, Nirban had asked him to come for some work.

'The book you are reading, do you like it? Or are you just leafing through it?'

They were in Nirban's room on the second floor, just the two of them. The afternoon was turning a shade of pink, the sky beginning to resemble cotton candy. As usual, there was a match going on outside Nirban's window. Football. Pushkar used to take a keen interest in the sport when Maradona was still playing. After the latter's retirement, he, too, was out of it, all that was left was the poster of the star on his wall. Pushkar, Maradona and time. Pushkar had read two pages of the book and kept it aside, it was too difficult. He has never read writing such as this, not even in Bengali. When he hesitantly confessed as much to Nirban, the latter replied, 'So what? Take your time. All good things need time. And the number of books I have, it will take you a few years to finish them all. Take them to read. But you do have to return them.'

Nirban flashed his trusting and boyish smile as he finished, just as a fight broke out in the field outside, perhaps due to the young referee's refusal to award a corner.

'What will you do after your studies?'

Nirban asked the question while leafing through a book he had taken off the bookshelf. Pushkar had never

faced this question, truth be told not even from his parents.
Perhaps they assumed he would end up doing something or
the other. Perhaps they thought he was going to be a singer or
a writer. Considering these were the two professions he was
familiar with at home, he would find recourse in either of the
two. Pushkar has learnt singing from his mother and from his
maternal uncle. If there are no music classes at home, at times
he sits by himself with the tanpura. And he writes in secret in
his diary within the privacy of his room. The tanpura and the
pen, possibly he will be drawn to one of these at some point,
but it's not something he likes to dwell on much. Possibly it's
not going to be either of those but something else entirely.
This is Pushkar's only source of relief, that his parents are in
no hurry to see him settle down. As if he has been brought to
the park to play and his parents are not interested in getting
home any time soon. As if they are on their way to catch a
train but have gotten too enamoured of the station itself. So
Pushkar remained quiet for a while, but eventually answered,
'I have not thought about it.'

Nirban took out the book he was looking for and brushed
off the dust on its cover as he spoke. 'Great! Keep doing that.
Don't think about it. It's no rule that everyone must have a
fixed plan about this. But don't stop writing. You have it in
you, don't let it go.'

Despite being of the same age, Nirban said things like
that from such a lofty position of experience and with such
earthy sincerity that it never failed to surprise Pushkar. He
was a writer himself, but he was so immersed in his work as
an editor that it seemed it was that persona which spoke out
the most.

'Let's go, Pushkar, there's no one else coming today.
You and I will visit the press. We will sit there and check the

third proofs. You will see the place as well. We must seriously get busy with work for the journal after this, isn't it?'

Nirban took out a white envelope from within the pages of the book he had just brought out. Inside it was money, the leaves visible from a distance. Dead.

'Money keeps well when you keep it inside a book. We have to pay the press today, let's go.'

They set out. Pushkar's curiosity at the prospect of seeing the press was shaken a little when they got off the metro and found themselves in Sovabazar. Nirban's house was in the south, near Netaji Nagar. Taking the other exit route led to Bansdroni, where Abhijit lived. Pushkar had assumed the press would be somewhere nearby. So, when they travelled along almost the whole of Kolkata to land up in Sovabazar, Pushkar was quite surprised. There was, however, a lot more left for him to be surprised about when Nirban led him past circuitous alleys and bylanes into a certain neighbourhood.

Pushkar had only read about this place in books or heard about it in conversations among friends. And it's not as if he had heard particularly respectful mentions of the area either. Rather, those accounts were always a mix of dismissive hatred and snide, amused indifference, like deliberately over-spicing food while cooking.

As they walked down one alley after another, Pushkar kept looking around him, more so because it seemed to him that every time they turned a corner in these narrow lanes, the personality of the neighbourhood changed. The kind of roads, the kind of houses, the faces at the doors and by the windows, the prints on the curtains hanging outside, how the shops were adorned, the fleeting gazes of passers-by, how they were talking, sounds heard in the distance, everything. It was all shifting at every corner. As if the narrow winding alleys were veins connecting the frantic city of Kolkata outside with a vastly different world within. In a while, just as dusk was about to settle, the two of them arrived at the heart of this world. Sonagachi.

The rickety slum around the square they were in seemed like it wanted to lean further towards the earth. From inside the ancient houses with sunken cheeks, crooked chins and eyes bulging out; through the doors and windows, red, blue and green fairy lights were bleeding out on to the road. Girls, women were stepping out of these doors, the blurry glow of their loud make-up flooding the nooks and crannies of the ramshackle locality. The lamps were decked with the dead fragrance of their flowers as Haarkata Gully began to wake up right in front of their eyes, in the evening, like a different world.

Pushkar did not say anything then, but Nirban understood the unspoken question colouring his astonished face and said, 'You must be thinking, why so far from our place? Even if it's far, why here? The thing is, this is where Pradip-da's press is. His house is here too. There are many people who live in this locality who work totally different jobs. Pradip-da is one such person. A friend had recommended him to me. We had no money back then, but we were mad about getting the journal out. When every press was slamming their door shut on our faces, it was Pradip-da who agreed to help us. He printed the edition without charging us a dime. Twice in a row. Now we have so many members, we make do via crowdfunding, but we have not managed to let go of Pradip-da. Our journal wouldn't exist if it weren't for him.'

Walking furtively ahead they reached the base of the stairs leading up to Pradip-da's press. A damp yard with a water tap on the side and a couple of lodgings. A narrow, slippery flight of stairs led up to the first floor. There, one could both smell the press and hear it. Pushkar spoke a little hesitantly, 'I should have asked you about the contribution.'

Nirban slapped him on the shoulder and said, laughing, 'Rubbish! You're new, why will you pay? Not this time. We'll work on the next edition around Pujo. Contribute then.'

That was a relief for Pushkar. Pujo was a good time, Baba would be getting his bonus. Ma's programmes happened only in the winter. But Baba would be getting a bonus, not much but still. This time, instead of clothes he would ask for money.

'Here, your new poet's poem.' Pradip-da hands them a paper from the printer without once turning his face from the screen. Pushkar takes the paper and glances at it.

Warm. New. Letters. Words. Language. Script. Print. Poem. His.

What exactly is this feeling, even he cannot tell. He could scarcely have imagined seeing his work in this manner, that he will be handed proofs to check, for it to be published in a journal—after so many rejections he had stopped believing that these things could ever be real. So today, on this stunned afternoon, all he can do is quietly sit for a moment, holding the still warm printed page containing his works.

'Is it okay if I check this at home? I was in a bit of a hurry today,' he enquires softly.

'It's just a few lines . . . Why do you need to take it home? Check it here!' Nirban replies.

Pushkar tries to explain to him that he wants to spend time with this poem, spend the commute with it and the night as well. Instead, he remains silent.

'Alright, fine. Take it home, but tomorrow you must bring it back yourself. That's fine, right? Day after is page release.'

Pushkar nods in acceptance and walks out on to the street. Nirban would be staying back to check the proofs of his long essay no matter how late it gets. It would be difficult figuring these lanes out in the evening, but Pushkar knows it will not be the right call to make it later. It has started drizzling, in the meanwhile. The area is livelier now, the narrow, secret conclaves sending a spiral of heat through his body, the radiance of the wares on display searing his soul.

A girl stares at him, standing at the threshold of one of the yawning doors, leaning against the rose-print curtains. He sees her looking at him. Noticing it, he lowers his gaze, but then raises it again, to figure out if she really is looking. *Yes, she is.* She is combing her hair, in a manner so leisurely it's as if someone is taking a history class or a ship is leaving a harbour. She is looking at him directly, perhaps to gauge his interest or lack thereof. In the guise of putting the sheet of paper in his bag and fishing an umbrella out, Pushkar lowers his eyes and glances inside his jhola, only to find it full of darkness. The uneasy darkness of this neighbourhood.

Just like the kind of darkness, fluid and sticky, that sticks to the flat and round disks of the printer in the printing section of Abanish's office. At night, this contraption will begin working over reels of swiftly rolling raw paper, when the newspaper will go to print. Abanish is on the veranda, the long one right outside the press overlooking the road flowing past far below. Earlier, this office used to be in North Kolkata, it's been a few years that they have shifted to the seventh floor of this fourteen-storey building in Mullick Bazar. Next to the building stretches the narrow length of Elliot Road, while the expanse of Mullick Bazar is in the front. One can spend hours gazing at this view from the balcony, although today it's not time that Abanish wishes to overcome here but, rather, his anxieties. He is a man of medium height and has a solid build, with curly salt-and-pepper hair, light glasses and a moustache. He is dressed in a brown khadi kurta with buttons on the sleeves and a pair of white pyjamas. There's a dot pen tucked in his pocket and a jhola which is at present lying on his desk as he steps out to light his filterless cigarette. He is the joint subeditor of the newspaper, but today he has not touched a single copy since evening.

The owners and the union are in a meeting on the eleventh floor; everyone is anxious to know the outcome. Apparently, profit margins have hit rock bottom; there's talk of a transfer of ownership, among other things. The union has been asking for this meeting for a long time and today they have managed to have their way. It's the twenty-third of the month and not a single employee has received their salary yet.

This side, it has begun to pour heavily. Abanish senses a light pressure on his shoulder. Suhrid. Suhrid Dasgupta, an exceptional poet, a junior in his desk. Suhrid, too, lights up a cigarette.

'The meeting's over, Abanish-da. Did you hear?'

'Oh, really?' Abanish snaps out of his daze. 'What was decided then?'

'This month we must manage somehow. There's no salary. They will regularize it from next month. At least that's what they have said. And they will add this month's salary to the Pujo bonus. However, they might drop the Pujo special edition this year. Let's see.'

'Oh, then this month . . .'

'No, nothing.'

From that sliver of a balcony on the seventh floor it seems to Abanish that the winding roads below are getting entangled with each other in the rain. As if someone wanted to tie a braid but got stuck and it all got entwined. The red signal of Mullick Bazaar looks smudged in the rain, the glow wavers. As if someone has lovingly smeared the bindi on the forehead of the girl with the tangled braid. Past the sound of the rain Abanish can hear Ishita's voice, somewhere far away . . .

Latt uljhi suljha ja balam … Mathe ki bindiya bikhar gayi hai.

This month's Bihag.

7

'See, isn't this a surprise?'

As Saheli asks him the question, a smirk lingering on her lips, Pushkar is acutely aware that, at this very moment, she is the object of scrutiny of all his friends and acquaintances and almost everyone in college, either directly or covertly. Their curiosity regarding new things would have yielded far more fruitful results if applied to their work, he thinks in irritation.

Although this truly was a surprise when, while leaving after finishing their practical classes on the third floor, he found Saheli where the wide corridor outside their department takes a turn, standing by herself and staring out into the distance. Sometimes Pushkar finds it difficult to bear the burden of a heart that fills with the same kind of joy no matter when he gets to see Saheli, a joy that is too excessive to bear. She is the same person he has known since Class VIII. That was when Saheli had transferred to Pushkar's school; he has known her since. Known her from a distance though, as they were in separate sections. Like moonlight casting border lines through villages at night, just as subtly boys and girls would be segregated into separate sections and classes right till their high-school exams.

It was only once when they were in Class XI that Pushkar really began to *see* her. They got acquainted, talked, shared food and time, learnt about each other's feelings. And that is how he figured out that other scary thing, the thing that makes him so happy. Love has this sense of fear, a wispy little feeling, which is very comforting. That fear is what Pushkar now carries with him all the time, somewhere within his curly hair-covered head, where light might not breach but love still does. What he cannot understand any more is how he has managed to not confess his feelings to her till date. He, however, knows that perhaps because he has not told her about his feelings that there still remains a kind of grace and equality between the two of them. He has remained silent about his feelings not because he is afraid this equation will break, but because he is anxious that it might change.

Should he say something today, when the sunlight has died down past noon and clouds are overcast on the expanse of the sky, when the colour all around resembles the hue of someone's beloved cheeks just before they start to weep, would that be the right time to tell her everything? As these thoughts cross his mind on seeing her, Pushkar almost runs to the corner of the veranda. Only the tree, the milkwood tree, knows about his love. Plus Abhijit suspects something, and rightly so. But has Saheli herself become aware of this even after sharing their gradually deepening connection over the past three years? Does this girl with specks of brown in her black, wavy hair know about it? The one with the square glasses that make her look like a teacher? Does she know? Is the girl with the blood-hued, composed and slender lips not aware of it at all? He runs up to her as the thought passes.

'So, isn't this a surprise?' she repeats herself.

'It sure is. I'm seriously surprised. You? All of a sudden? In our college?'

'Why? Is it prohibited to enter your college? Can't I come?'

'Of course you can! You've never come before, which is why I asked.'

'Fine. Here I am today. If I had come earlier, would you have been surprised like this?'

'No, there's no way but accepting defeat in the face of such incredible logic.'

'They declared a half-day in our college today, someone passed away. So, I thought I'd come over.'

'That's great! We also have two periods off today. We have class again at 4.15 p.m.'

'It's so strange, isn't it? Someone I didn't know passed away and here I am celebrating that holiday by visiting you. I didn't know the person, and neither will I get to know them. Yet their death has given me an entire afternoon off.'

'Don't think of it that way. Things in the world are connected like this; if you dwell on it, you will feel sad. I don't.'

'You know what it is? Habit. Everything is habit. Like how we are all in different colleges, but I still feel like seeing you for a bit every day. Doesn't happen as frequently, so here I am. At least for today. But listen, don't tell Asmita I was here. It's different if we run into her because otherwise if she hears later, she will be hurt. But today I'm here only for you.'

'Rest assured, I won't tell. I don't meet Asmita too often either. These days, she stays a little aloof. Who knows . . . anyway.'

'So, you're free till 4.15?'

'Absolutely. Do you want to go and have some tea?'

'I don't want to go to the canteen.'

'Their tea is terrible anyway. Plus it's always crowded. In the next lane there's this woman who runs a stall, she makes very good tea. I hope you don't mind siting outside on someone's porch?'

'You know me. I don't mind sitting on the floor either.'

'Let's go then.'

Saheli leads the way, Pushkar trailing in her wake. They climb down the dimly lit winding staircase of the third floor to reach the ground below. It seems to Pushkar that suddenly there are more stairs than other days, it's taking them longer. As if someone has stretched out the stairs like a twisted spring and so the time trapped within the stairs has stretched out as well. No one other than him senses this, the rest are going up and down as usual.

Saheli is in an expensive maroon skirt with multicoloured Rajasthani motifs and a light-green top, the front buttons of which are pink, like tiny eyes. And yet as she climbs down the stairs ahead of him, all he can see is her in a white saree with a blue border, like all these years. A habit. All of it.

'Maasi, two black teas please. Make it well. She is a school friend, don't let my college's reputation get tarnished!'

Relieved by the woman's shy smile and the sight of her putting her bent-out-of-shape saucepan on with water, Pushkar sits down on the bench on the opposite side, with Saheli beside him. This road goes right by their college up to Harish Mukherjee Road. There aren't too many cars, but college students can always be found in the lane.

'Wait. Let me return your property to you.'

Saheli fishes Pushkar's red diary out from her bag and hands it to him, as if returning the keys to some secret treasure that she has not stolen but has enjoyed to her heart's content. Clutching the diary, Pushkar notices her hands, barely touching each other as they are placed delicately on her knees, as if they have frozen before they could transform into wings. Pushkar glances furtively at those hands, from her fingers to her wrist, to her elbow and then her arms. Like he has many times before. Some cloud in some corner shifts a little and a shaft of dying sunlight falls on one of her arms. What he has wanted to do for so many years, an errant ray of sunlight does with no trouble. It's holding her hand. Something Pushkar has not managed to do, despite wanting to, in so many years, out of uncertainty and doubt. He has never taken her hand in his, never known the taste of her touch, its fragrance and hue. And an unknown sun is doing this very thing right in front of him. From her slender, wheat-toned, rounded wrists, past the turn of her elbow right up to her upper arm, there are five moles on her over this long distance. Black, bright. Worthy of admiration. Confident. And this unknown, dying sunlight is grazing her arms in such a manner today that to Pushkar it seems it's not the sunlight at all. As if far away in some kitchen, the fresh, vibrant sunlight has been cooked and boiled down to this mild soup, which has then been ladled on to her skin bit by bit, and like the moles, the nigella seeds have floated to the surface. *How would this sunny soup taste?*

'What is it? Why are you staring at my hands? Tell me something . . .'

Startled out of his stupor and embarrassed, Pushkar speaks up somehow.

'What do you mean . . . did you read them? My work?'

'Yes, I did. Stayed up through the night. My parents must be wondering how much I am studying.'

'If they ever find out it's from my diary of poems, I will never be able to set foot in your place again.'

'The opposite might happen as well. Maybe they'll be more welcoming if they find out you're a budding poet.'

'Budding poet. That's well put. Feels nice hearing it.'

'Now it's just me, soon everyone else will also be saying it. Mark my words.'

'It's these word balloons of yours that have caused me all the trouble. No one else says these things. Not that too many know either, there's just Abhijit. Who will read my poems, who will even consider me an up-and-coming poet? Most of my work is rejected by publishers, nothing is ever published.'

'You don't write just to get it published, do you?'

'No, it's not that . . .'

'Then?'

'Only Abhijit and you are my readers. If you two consider me a budding poet, then I'm fine with it.'

'See, I believe everything has a right time. I don't believe in destiny, but I do believe in time. Time exists and it has its unique conditions. Were we born on this earth in three or four months? No, we were not . . . no one was. It takes nine months. Why? That's it, that's time. If you sow the seeds of a flowering plant in your garden today, water it and take care of it, will it still be able to bear flowers in a week? No, it's going to take exactly the amount of time needed for flowers to bloom. It's the same with your poetry. Now only two people know about it. Like when a baby is about to be born, it's usually the family and the doctor who get to know first. Perhaps it's not time yet for others to know about it.

However, one day the time will come, I know this. And I'm not saying this just because you are my friend. When I read these poems at night, alone, in the light of the table lamp, I can visualize a poet of the future, my friend. In that future, I cannot say for certain where we will be, but I can always see clearly how these words of yours, imprisoned within the pages of your diary, have reached numerous readers. But we must wait. I know it's natural to feel hurt when faced with rejection. Rejection breaks people, especially if it has been happening for a long time. But as a friend, I will ask you to wait, to be patient. Because I know you have the courage to wait, because I know you. It's not the right time yet for these pieces, that is why they have been rejected. One day they will not be returned, they will be accepted and then you will know that the time has come. However, be it today or that day, you will still be writing for yourself. You are your own biggest reader and you must reach your own self with this writing. And you can do that, can't you?'

A spoon in the small glass stirs a storm in the tea, white, sugary foam swirling and gravitating towards the turbulence in the centre. It's steaming hot and Saheli lightly blows into it. The tea can't be sipped now. But it's still ready and waiting to get cold.

Wait. Time. Wait. Time. Space. Word. Space. Word. Space. Wait. Space.

Pushkar has no answer to all these words said in one go. There is no answer to be given. Neither will there ever be such a friend who can explain things in such a way. But he does have such a friend. Saheli. His friend. His confidante.

The clouds that have gathered today are all bark and no bite, Pushkar already sensed this. There will be no rain today. For a long time the two of them sit there, side by side, sipping tea and watching the traffic drift by. After a while, Saheli gets up to leave.

'I must get going. I will drop by Disha's on my way back. She is really unwell, and I have to give her a couple of books.'

'Let's go, I'll walk you to the metro.'

'Why will you go all the way and then back? Your classes will begin soon. Get inside. I'll call you tomorrow.'

Even her refusals are so sweet that they are difficult for him to turn down, Pushkar wonders, still holding his diary of poems in his left hand. Suddenly, Saheli gathers up his free right hand in both of hers. He has waited for this for so many years but never managed to muster enough courage for it, and today it has finally happened without any preparation. However, he has no time or occasion to dwell on the thought. All he can do is to try and absorb the heated touch and warm taste of her hold with his own scrawny, unprepared hand and assure himself that this moment is indeed real.

She holds on to his hand for a moment longer and then presses it ever so lightly before letting go, like a bracket falling and separating a number from its chain. Then she glances at him and says, 'Your writing must happen.'

As she disappears amid the swirling crowd with these parting words, everything seems to change. There is no going back to class, no going to visit Pradip-da to submit the proofs after this. Somehow, Pushkar manages to push himself into an empty bus travelling towards his locality. Time, again, seems to have lengthened. Because the way back home from college seems longer. As if a large stretch of this pitched road that was kept rolled up like a carpet all this time has been unfurled today, extending the commute as well. By the time he reaches his neighbourhood, it's late, perhaps past midnight. All at once, he discovers that gravity does not seem to be working in these parts today.

Two cats float past him towards Lukkai's house.

All the deuce balls, cambric balls and footballs lost in the garden of Seema's house over the years have soared up in the air and are spinning all around. Five cambric balls and two deuce balls around one football, like a tiny moving solar system.

The doors of their house are ajar. A few tanpuras and a single pen are swirling around in the outer room. Chhutki is floating serenely.

He notices Ma, fast asleep and up in the air, the drape of her saree trail long behind her like a shadowy path to somewhere.

Baba is not asleep. Papers are up in the air, Baba and his table are airborne as well. As is the dim lamp on the table. Baba is still writing, his words floating on the surface of the page in front of him.

Throughout the house, utensils, ladles, spoons, *kadhai*s, spatulas, cups and dishes are twirling in the air.

Dodging it all Pushkar wades through the air and drifts into his room. They have a floating house, with floating light and darkness. His parents' old love is afloat in the air. Their present quarrels are too. Him as well. As he enters his room, he realizes it is completely covered in snow. He had forgotten to close the window before leaving. On his bed, on his writing table, on the chairs, on the switchboards are layers and layers of snow everywhere. White. Flaky. Deep.

All of a sudden, his diary escapes his grasp and takes flight. Its cover comes off and a small, folded note falls out into the air. Somehow Pushkar manages to push his way to it and catch hold of it.

The snow melts immediately.

Every floating thing touches the ground.

Slowly, the night morphs into evening.

Pushkar unfolds the piece of paper in his hand. It is not a note. It is an entire letter.

Saheli's letter.

8

Gunjan steps out on to his tiny veranda. The last batch of the day has left a while ago, all that remains now around him is a bit of fatigue. The fact that this fatigue is a bit more than what most people his age feel is something Gunjan can tell. In front of him, a narrow road leads away to the distance, like it always has. Gunjan is fascinated by roads, he always observes them at length when he sees one. He is surprised because he feels so many people travel over roads, but the roads never go anywhere. When he takes classes in college or at home, he feels the same about poetry, as if that, too, is a kind of a road. Not just the ones he teaches from the syllabus but also in the larger world of poetry outside, he finds each poem to be a unique little road in itself. That is how Gunjan feels. Gunjan, who has grown more tired and quieter over time. This is how he feels about poetry. Different readers can travel to different destinations with the same text. What an incredible art form! Not just poetry, cinema, painting and many of the other arts behave in much the same way. The form is fixed, but through them, the reader or the audience is transported elsewhere. The same poem that might take Gunjan somewhere, might take someone else much further. This is something Gunjan is certain of. Nothing is more relative than the meaning of a poem. The narrow road up ahead, beside which lies an even more silent little pond, seems to Gunjan to be a slender poem as well.

His smoking has gone up these days, especially after the students leave. He keeps lighting up one after the other and goes on talking to himself. Things he never ended up telling anyone, things he always wanted to say. At such times, he feels he is a different person and finds himself facing his own image. It stands across him and listens to him, talks to him. He can also appreciate how difficult it is to have to listen to himself quietly. He will be sixty soon, the age for his retirement is drawing closer. What all is he to retire from? This heavy title of a retiree that people earn, other than their job, what other things do they manage to retire from? Gunjan does want to step down, but not from work. Rather, he knows that it will be a lot more difficult for him if he stops teaching.

Near his feet, on the mosaic floor bathed in moonlight, lies the bundled-up morning newspaper, never picked up. It never is, usually Mitali puts it away the next day while wiping the floor. It is never picked up, opened or read. It is still delivered though, only to find itself abandoned in the balcony. Habit. Today, Gunjan notices the newspaper, he has never seen one in the moonlight. He bends over to pick it up from the mosaic floor gleaming under the light of the moon and, instead of the paper, comes back up with a tiny doll that had fallen on the ground a little while ago. A little more than seven years, to be precise.

'What is this, Parama? Don't vent your anger on her dolls.'

'What else should I do? What is the point of expressing my anger at humans in this house? What proof do I have that human beings are not puppets as well?'

'I don't want to fight at this hour of the night, Parama. Please, Pupey is sleeping in the other room. She has school in the morning. Please, not now.'

'So, when do you want to fight, Gunjan? Tell me! Let me note the date and the time.'

'Don't be so sarcastic.'

'At least you still get the sarcasm, if nothing else.'

'You know I never want to fight.'

'It does not work like that, Gunjan. The moment I try to say something, have a discussion, you think it is a fight. You have stopped talking to me because you are afraid it will be a fight. Do you get that? Do you feel it? A relationship does not work like this.'

'It's not that, Parama. We are both busy with our own work. Plus with Pupey . . .'

'Speak for yourself, Gunjan. You are busy with your work. I am as well but only at certain times. After I get back from the bank, my entire world is you two. But where are you in that world? After college you have batches and batches of tuition. I get it, you love teaching. Then what? Then you are with a book at your table. There is a book in front of you at dinner. Forget about me, do you have any idea how much Pupey misses you?'

'I will try, Parama, I will. I understand it gets difficult for you. But . . .'

'No buts, Gunjan. The thing is, you avoid the world outside your books. You are afraid of it, you don't want to get into it. That's fine, but you should have thought about all that before. Before your marriage, before our courtship. Back then you had time for me, now you don't, not for anyone. Sometimes it feels like I am here simply because I just am, but you are not there with me. You are with Tennyson, Wordsworth, Yeats and Baudelaire. They are the ones you talk to, deal with, eat with and sleep with. But they all are sleeping in their graves, Gunjan. That is where you have dragged our relationship as well.'

Gunjan stood there quietly, leaning against the wall. There was a lamp in the room and moonlight on the floor of the veranda. Two different worlds—it was important to distinguish between the inside and the outside. This argument, this dispute was tiring him out. In his heart he knew everything she was saying was true, she was sitting on the bed with warm tears rolling down her face. He should go to her. At least he should hand her the napkin in his pocket. But he could not. Something took hold of him, like the wind takes hold of a tree.

'You have nothing to say, do you? Not even this time.'

Her voice was low as she wiped away her tears. Gunjan's tired head dipped a little more, but he still did not say anything.

'Can you explain this letter to me?'

Gunjan raised his head to find Parama pull out a white envelope from under her pillow. With his name and college address written on it in English. He knew the letter, knew it very well. And he knew this would only add fuel to fire. But it could no longer be avoided by keeping quiet either.

'You know what it is, Parama. Why unnecessarily . . .'

'Unnecessarily? This is unnecessary for you, Gunjan? You do not want to accept the offer, fine. That is your decision. But you did not consider telling me about it even once? You did not even tell me you have declined it. Does that mean I feature nowhere in your life?'

'It's not that, Parama. I do not want to move somewhere new at this age, leaving the college, this house, this city. The time it takes to get used to life abroad, I want to dedicate that time to my studies. I had sent them a paper long back for comments. Back then, I had an interest in attending these workshops. There was no response from them at that time, and I could scarcely have imagined they would remember it after these years and make me such an offer. Five years is a long time, Parama. I do not have the same drive regarding these workshops either. Rather, there is a lot of work to be done right here, many more things to be read.'

'Oh! So, all that is not possible at Princeton, is it? Is that what you want to say? What is the matter with you? You did not think it necessary to consult me even once before turning down such an offer? If I were not cleaning out your desk, I would have never found out that they have sent you an offer for an International Language Workshop with an honorary lectureship at Princeton, where writers and academics from thirty countries are invited, and you never even replied to them. I know you have a job here. But would you not have gotten a lien easily for this? This could be a feather in your cap. Not only did you turn it down, you also never told me about it. How do you explain this? Put yourself in my shoes, Gunjan, and ask yourself this.'

Gunjan took a deep breath. Like a footballer about to take a corner shot just before the final whistle, or a patient about to be put under anaesthetics, or even a novelist about to write the concluding line.

'Perhaps we should not clean out each other's desks, Parama. That way our lives will be cleaner as well.'

Parama was silent for a long while. When she spoke, her voice sounded different. 'What exactly are you trying to say?'

'I don't want to say anything, Parama. Saying everything out loud disrupts the balance of life. For everyone. So, it's best not to say anything.'

'It does not work like that, Gunjan. If the topic has come up, finish it. What do you want to say?'

It was the end of winter, and the fans were off. So Gunjan's sigh was audible before he spoke. 'Five years ago, I found two white envelopes from your desk as well. I was looking for matches. Since you smoke occasionally, I was looking through your desk. I should not have.'

In the darkness Parama's shadow was still. That's how she remained for a while. Then she asked, 'Which two envelopes?'

'The first from the fertility clinic we had been visiting. Results of my sperm count, that it was zero. I was never going to be a father. A report that never reached me, rather it was explained to me that everything was all right. We must keep on trying. The second one from Bombay, Sayantan's letter. Declaring his happiness at the news of your pregnancy. That he could not meet you because he was flying abroad, but that he was willing to make all necessary arrangements for his child.'

A piece of glass slowly embedding itself in a butterfly's wings, colour and not blood spurting out.

Someone leaping for their dreams with a parachute on, but it refuses to open.

A pair of hands slowly sewing up an apple. The skin on the apple swelling with the mark of the threads.

Rows and rows of empty vases placed on the sand in a desert at night.

Two pigeons refusing to fly away even after the door to the cage is left open.

A dying ship.

'I can explain.'

'I have not asked for any, Parama. Not in these five years. Neither will I in the future. But yes, perhaps for that I will need to shield myself with a lot more books. You are right. I am afraid of the outside world, afraid of questions and their answers. Our desks are compartments of our lives. Space. Entering that space can upset this delicate balance. I used to be afraid of this very thing. But it could not be avoided.'

'But why don't you want any explanations, Gunjan? Don't you love me even a little bit any more? Even such a huge incident makes no difference to you. You won't even let me explain.'

'Explaining the past yields no benefits, Parama, except wasting time. It has happened somehow. Besides, there were many faults and shortcomings on my part too. I did not give you time, I could not give you a child either. So, I am no one to demand answers. But yes, I should not have opened the desk. Since then, there have been two white envelopes between us. Today there's just one more.'

'But for Pupey you are . . .'

'I know. She is not involved in this. In fact, even those two envelopes never came between the two of us.'

'I know. You have given it your all as a father. I have nothing to say there. I wish none of this had happened. But back then—'

'Please, Parama, don't. I don't want to know.'

'Fine. But someday I will tell you. Even if you don't want to know. Because it is my burden to tell you. But Pupey will only know you as her father as long as I am alive. All I have left to say today is that I have received an offer as well, from Bangalore. It's a big job, a huge hike. I want to accept it. I have not replied to them, did not want to do it without talking to you. But here everything is suffocating me a little. I need some space. Perhaps you do too.'

'And Pupey?'

Gunjan glances at the doll. It has become a rolled-up newspaper again. It seems it takes a doll seven years to become a newspaper. Exactly a month after that night, the day they were set to leave for Bangalore and Pupey was clutching him tightly and weeping, he had unzipped her backpack and slipped in a piece of paper before kissing her and whispering in her ear, 'You will understand when you are all grown up, okay?'

Pupey has grown up a little now. At least by seven more years. Grown up enough for a doll to turn into paper. Turning back towards the room, Gunjan walks up to the bookshelf and takes out a book. Written by one of those people he has been living with all these years. William Butler Yeats.

> My mind, because the minds that I have loved,
> The sort of beauty that I have approved,
> Prosper but little, has dried up of late,
> Yet knows that to be choked with hate
> May well be of all evil chances chief.
> If there's no hatred in a mind
> Assault and battery of the wind
> Can never tear the linnet from the leaf.
> An intellectual hatred is the worst,
> So let her think opinions are accursed.
> Have I not seen the loveliest woman born
> Out of the mouth of Plenty's horn,
> Because of her opinionated mind
> Barter that horn and every good
> By quiet natures understood
> For an old bellows full of angry wind?

He finishes reading the poem and sits quietly for a while. 'A Prayer for My Daughter'. Has she read the entire poem by now? He hears her voice over the phone from time to time. Sometimes he feels like writing her a letter but cannot bring himself to do it. Perhaps he will someday.

He is out of cigarettes. It's past eleven, but Bapi's shop would still be open on the other side of the lake. It had stopped raining a while back, only the air feels a bit damp now. Gunjan puts on his slippers and sets out. Usually he is at his desk at this hour with a book, that goes on until late. Tonight, he is out after ages. However, before he can reach Bapi's shop, he comes abruptly to a halt at the sight of the lake. He cannot explain why. He usually does not look for answers to the whys all the time, he just goes with it. So, he stops. There is no one in sight, just a few parked rickshaws here and there. Trees surround the placid and silent rectangular lake, which looks like it wants to swell up a bit more this monsoon. A few steps lead down to the ghat and then the water below. The water is now awash with moonlight, as if concealing something forbidden underneath it, something that must not be known.

Gunjan stands there for a long time. The air has a certain coldness to it. He begins to remember a few lines of a poem, not from among the foreign poets who occupy much of his days. In the depth of the night he is reminded of a few lines by poet Jibanananda Das, written in Bengali:

. . . the gesture that fells even stars,
They leave the soft blue bosom of the sky
And sink below the frost,
Silver paddy that falls in the mist one day;
Perhaps scops owls will sing their song in the dark.

Gunjan remains standing there, the lines churning in his head. In the forbidden space between the water and the moonlight.

9

'So, you did not go yesterday to submit the proofs? Should you not be a little more serious?'

Today Kakima has mixed the moori with pickle oil, its heat and smell repeatedly hitting the nose. Mango pickle oil, a little bit of peanuts, some *chanachur* and a sprinkling of chopped green chillies. The tea will be here any moment, Pushkar knows. He also knows there will be some choice words from Abhijit. A little while ago, Nirban ran into Abhijit and complained to him with a grave expression that Pushkar has not gone and submitted the final proofs at the printers' as decided. The journal is set to go to print tomorrow afternoon, for which Nirban will have to visit the press in the morning to check out the tracing. Pushkar must go and hand the proofs over to Nirban and do them all a favour. If Pradip-da has to prepare a fresh page make-up and tracing, Nirban would have to handle all the trouble. Nevertheless, he wants, that too quite sincerely, to include Pushkar's poem in the volume.

Having realized the delicacy of the situation, Pushkar decides to tell the truth.

'Saheli came to see me at college suddenly yesterday. I don't know what happened after that, I just did not feel like going to the press.'

Pushkar can sense the annoyed look on Abhijit's face even in the darkness of the balcony where the same cassette is playing on the tape recorder. Suman Chattopadhyay. 'The further, the further you go, friend, it is the same pain.' It's not untrue, but he cannot recall if he has ever heard something like that in a song. Suman has songs about it, his advice is that one shouldn't go very far. Nonetheless, everything seems to be going out of hand at present.

'See, this is between Saheli and you. But the press is not going to wait for you. Try and understand this. I took you to them. I have some credibility, at least think about that even if you don't think about yours!'

'Alright, don't worry. I will drop by Nirban's on my way back from here. I have the proof with me. In fact, I did not want to part with it. It's my first one after all.'

'This city is witness to all my firsts, the more it pursues me, the more I flee'—a new song begins playing on the cassette player. First proofs should be counted among the other firsts, shouldn't it?

'Did you tell her anything? Or did you just take back the diary?'

'I will write poems or confess, I can't do both.'

'You think she reads your poems and gets it?'

'Perhaps she does.'

'How do you know? Did she tell you?'

'Don't get so worked up about confessions all the time, Abhijit. I know you confessed your love for Asmita. Although it was she who made the first move, I know that too. How did it turn out?'

Abhijit falls silent at the question. He has just picked up a handful of moori, which he lets go. They fall back into the bowl, like boys rushing on to a field.

'Yes, she did, three years back. Do you remember the day?'

'How can I forget? You and I, Asmita and Saheli, we had walked to the bus stop after school when suddenly it began to rain torrentially. Saheli was in a hurry to get to her tuition, so she braved the rain to get on the next bus. I could see there was something brewing between the two of you, for which you had to be left alone. I made up some excuses and walked into the stationery shop nearby so I could surreptitiously keep watch. Asmita's head was lowered, you took her hand in yours and said your piece for a long time. I could not help but feel that the rain was very important to both of you.'

Suman continues to sing on the tape. Abhijit remains quiet a while longer and then finally speaks.

'You say it like that because you are a romantic. Or because you write poetry. I know, be it rain or storm or sunshine, it would have ended up the same. Like what eventually happened.'

'See, love has faults, it can break. I can understand all that, even if it hurts I can. But the two of you love each other, you want to be together, but it will have to come to an end because people at home are not okay with it, that is something I just cannot accept. It is not for me. Not because I'm a romantic or I write poems, but because I just don't get it anyway.'

It's not clear if the words mollify Abhijit a little, but his tone softens. To be honest, it is difficult for Pushkar to explain how Abhijit can remain so calm and collected, at least on the surface, even after knowing the wedding plans being made at Asmita's house. Pushkar knows if it were him, he would not have been able to stay so calm. Although he is just as aware that he will probably not reach that far at all.

'I agree,' replies Abhijit. 'But now, even if we want to, we cannot get married, isn't it? We are both in our first year of college. We will both need at least four more years to find some work. I am counting our MA and MSc in this. There is nothing to be done without this time. Plus not everyone is the same. Asmita is quiet, docile. It's just not possible for her to revolt against her family. She has told them a few times, her sister has too. They have spoken about me as well. In fact, the last time we met, her father was on his way back in a rickshaw. He saw us and understood everything that was going on. Then there was a huge showdown at home. She has been asked to stop seeing me. There is nothing I can do unless she herself does something. But she won't be able to, I know that. So, I am not putting any pressure, at least not on her. On myself, I'm trying to be as stern as I can. That's it.'

There is very little food left in the bowl. Picking the last few crumbs up with his fingers, Pushkar declares, 'But I have not been asked to stay away from Asmita, have I?'

'What do you mean?'

'It's simple. Asmita and I are in the same college. Are you forgetting that? She is in English, I am in geography. She is on the first floor, I am on the second. She goes to college every day, so do I. We do not talk much, but now we will. We can meet after any period, her parents won't be there to watch over us.'

'What is the point? Just going to add to complications.'

'Not at all. I cannot do that either. All I will do is hand her a letter. Like a messenger.'

'Letter? What letter? Whose letter?'

'Obviously not a government appointment letter. Your letter. You are going to write to her, which I am going to deliver. There is no harm in trying one last time.'

'You are talking as if this is poetry. Will a letter be able to solve this problem? Is that even possible? Only she can speak up, go against her family. She is the one who must do it, nothing can be done from outside.'

'Perhaps she will be able to do it. But for that we need your letter. A letter that will give her the strength, show her your support, provide her courage. Not everyone can manage everything alone, you just said it yourself. You cannot call her now. Her family members will pick up the phone and they will not let you talk. The two of you cannot meet either. So, write this letter, one last time. Let me take it to her. If it works, it works. If not, then that'll be it. Agreed?'

Abhijit thinks for a moment and then replies, 'Alright. But my letters are not so impactful, let me tell you that.'

'You will be writing it, you won't know its strength. The person who reads it will know.'

Sometime after this conversation, Pushkar finds himself standing on the edge of the square field, all by himself. The games played on the field are over, only the dust lingers, alongside the patches where the grass is gone. Besides, there are two rickety goalposts and the traces of marks and grids made on the ground with chalk. Just two hours ago, this place was booming with excitement, now nothing remains.

On the other side of the field stands Nirban's house, confident, shapely, tall and three-storeyed. Two people are visible from the distance, walking back and forth on the roof, one professor of chemistry and another a student of English. Nirban's father and sister. Pushkar can also see the windows of Nirban's room where the light is on; Nirban is in bed, his head lowered, as if he is working on something. It is certain he did not finish proofreading his long article in one night. If he goes to see him now, Nirban will certainly scold him, so he pauses. He needs to be prepared before facing such a situation. Not that it matters in any significant way, but still.

His hand is in the pocket of his shirt. His fingers trace two letters folded inside. One he will hand over in a while, the other he hopes never to part with. He takes out the latter and unfolds it. The little time it takes to brace himself for the scolding, beside the field under the yellowish light of the lamp post, will be enough to finish reading Saheli's letter again. Although he has lost count of the number of times he has read it, he is sure to feel good if he reads it once again.

Pushkar,

I never thought I would write you a letter. But there are so many unexpected things that take place in our lives, things we never really thought would happen. This is something like that. So, I have dropped everything to write to you. We have been meeting every day all these years. Just for the sake of that, there are a few things I must tell you today. The thing is, not all friendships are the same, the inner workings of individual relationships cannot be same either. In the last few years, you have become the kind of friend with whom I can share anything and everything. Hence this letter. I do not know what you will think when you read this, but I feel lighter just writing it.

I know you are in love with me. It is not something I have figured out recently; I have always known it. I believe the kind of love where you do not have to say anything aloud, where you understand each other anyway, is much stronger than any other kind. That is how I have sensed your love. If you ask me to explain exactly how and when I found out, I don't think I will be able to. Nor do I wish to. But while spending time with you at addas, in school, on the road or at home, I have witnessed your love for me grow gradually even though you never said a word. And I knew you would never say anything, because that's how you are, that's how you are wired. Rather, you would say it all in your poetry like you do every day.

If I am to mention a bigger reason, then I will mention the poems you have written in the last two years, those diaries. I am closer to them than I am with you. Even when I have been absent from school and missed my classes, recess, the conversations with friends and even you, it is your poems that I have felt more strongly about. Even back then, I knew that you had your diary with you in your jhola and that it was full of pages of new writing. That the person who would get to read those after you would be me. So I felt terrible on the days I was not there. Can I tell you the truth? I do not know how much of it applies to you, but at least with your poems I have developed a sense of ownership. As if they are supposed to reach my eyes before they reach anyone else's. That I am supposed to read them before anyone else does. Perhaps this is silly, but it makes me feel good. Like it makes me feel good to imagine that one day your poems will go beyond your diary, spread far and wide, and many readers other than me will want to read them. Do not forget about me when that happens, okay?

See, what did I begin with and where have I ended up! Although it is natural since I am not a poet like you and cannot organize my thoughts properly. Remember that when you read this. As I was saying, it is your poetry that has revealed the most about your feelings for me. I have never been able to visualize myself this clearly anywhere as I can see myself in your poems. Not even in front of a mirror. And it is these poems that have told me day in, day out about your love for me. They have hidden nothing. Alas, if only everyone had such a weapon.

I don't know why you love me so much, but it is a nice feeling knowing I am this important to someone, that I am wanted. I don't know if you can sense it or if I will even be able to explain it to you, but I love you too. These days I hear so many people say things like, 'I love you but just as a friend.' Such words make me laugh just as much they make me angry. If you really love someone as a friend, then why is there a 'but'? Is it at all possible to love so much without being friends? I have no such things to say to you. You are my best friend, and it is you who I love the most. In every which way. However, even I have a 'but' here and that is why I am writing this letter to you.

When there is love between people, they often think of many things, like about being together, living under the same roof, having a child and so on. This is not a problem for me. However, this love that is so precious, so dear to me, a love that is so different, I do not want to tie it down with any single kind of a definition. I have often noticed how the larger world outside tends to get lost when one tries to contain it within four walls. I have seen the other way round as well, but much less so. Therefore I am afraid. I am afraid because deep down you and I are similar—restless,

sensitive, unorganized, scattered and crazy. To me, a home is
akin to a harbour: if one person is a ship, then the other has
to be an anchor. Calm, composed, organized and practical. I
need such an anchor in my life. Perhaps it is not evident, but
a feeling of uncertainty and edginess plagues me at all times.
I cannot live with such a feeling my entire life so I need an anchor.
And I never want to see you in that role because it is not meant for
you. You are a ship. Huge, powerful, capable of accommodating
many people, but still floating, not stationary. You belong in the
sea, in the open. Even if I am not a ship like you, at least assume I
am like a boat. Whenever you are sailing through the heart of the
ocean, if you see the sails of a tiny boat in the distance, then that
would be me. And I will be able to see you from the shore as well.

We will meet, we will keep meeting, mark my words. On the
water, in the tides. I will chat with you a while and then come
back ashore while you drift off somewhere far away again. That
is how our love will survive. Three quarters of this world is water,
one quarter is land. Our love will never fit into such a tiny space.
What do you say? When your poems reach a lot more people, only
if you wish to, let me read a few of them in advance, alright?
Do not take that away from me. You will remember that, right?
Be happy, a lot.

Saheli

Pushkar remains standing beside the field in the darkness
for a long time, calm and heavy waves from the heart of an
ocean lapping at his feet. Those who write letters scarcely
comprehend their impact. Those who read, do. He was not
wrong when he had said this to Abhijit.

10

When the golden light of dusk says, 'You are mine'
I see the red darkness slip off their face, into a cup,
Whether I raise the chalice to my lips or not
Ten horses from ten corners of existence race to the horizon.
Holding the sun's blood, I wait, unquenched,
No questions anywhere, no roads either
That I may walk down, one last time.
O Sun, cruel and capable
Does it not occur to you even once, this final evening
As you extinguish yourself
To take me with you?
Holding the sun's blood, I wait, unquenched—
Who am I? Who?
Ten horses from ten corners of existence race to the horizon
I hide my face in my own corner and weep.
Once, the last time.
Mercy? What do you call mercy?

Dark-green, bright-red and stark-yellow circles of light fall repeatedly on the rough, off-white, thin paper of the newsprint on which these lines are neatly written and arranged. As the eye moves from one letter to the next, the colour changes in a manner reminiscent of how people shift from one colour to another before elections. The thought crosses Suhrid's mind as he finishes the poem. Once, twice, thrice he traces the entire length of the poem as if reading an X-ray plate over light. This is what poetry is to him. Something that cannot be perceived from the outside but reveals immeasurable secrets when held under the light. Or else why write or read poems? So, every time Suhrid reads a poem, he tries to get past its outer shell and find his way within. Be it his own or someone else's, the deeper you go, the more rewarding it is.

At present, however, he finds it a tad difficult to find his way inside the poem, not only because of the stark changing lights but also because of a tone-deaf performance of a popular song being belted out, apparently the main draw that ensures a steady clientele in this tiny, seedy bar-cum-restaurant at this hour. Live Dance & Live Music, it is emblazoned on the door. In the evenings, those doors swing open to reveal this small place with the low ceilings lit by the red, blue and yellow lights. The singer in the distance seems faded in the haze of cigarette smoke, as if there is no way to reach out to her no matter how much one wishes. There is dancing here and something else too, something that starts a little later in the night when the unruly revelries of the patrons completely fill up Blue Light Bar. Suhrid Dasgupta does not like coming to this place much, but today he decided to accompany Abanish.

Abanish usually has a run-down air about him; seen approaching from a distance that ramshackle look becomes even more apparent to Suhrid. Except for a couple of people like Abanish, no one in their office truly appreciates how good a poet Suhrid is. He is a regular reader of all of Suhrid's books. In fact, it was Abanish who insisted Suhrid write for the Pujo special issue. Suhrid otherwise has no feelings left for his job except for the fact that it pays the bills. That Suhrid has an abiding respect for his more-than-fifty-years-old, broken senior colleague is not just because the man is one of his readers. Abanish has a surprising candour about him that Suhrid really appreciates. He is man who feels no shame in admitting the truth, especially regarding all his failures and shortcomings. This attitude scares Suhrid but also provides him courage. Besides, he loves Abanish and admires him and is just as fond and respectful of the broken bits. In this city, so many people want to be so many things, so many of them never make it, it amazes Suhrid. Like Abanish. He wanted to be a poet, became a journalist instead. Not that many people in the office know his secret, except Suhrid. So, from time to time, Abanish reads out some of his work to Suhrid, looking for some straightforward feedback. Suhrid never deceives him, he just shares his views as they are.

Like he chooses to do now. Abanish likes getting high, loves drinking. However, the drinking is no longer just recreational, it has become a need, a compulsion. Suhrid has been picking up on this for a while. He has noticed that Abanish's drinking has gone up ever since trouble began in their office, with the impasse between the owners and the union. Nowadays, whether he has money or not, Abanish always comes to this bar in the lane next to their office after work. Some days he even ends up borrowing money from his colleagues and it is really upsetting. Today Suhrid has decided to foot as much of the bill as he can.

'How does it sound, Suhrid?'

Abanish directs the question at him in a slightly slurry voice. His gaze is still clear, the cheap alcohol has not managed to alter it. Here, in this corner table of Blue Light Bar he has pulled out a sheet of paper from his bag and put it in front of Suhrid. It's been ten minutes.

'If I'm being honest, Abanish-da, the idea is excellent. The thought reflects current concerns, the images as well. But you must be more careful about your choice of words, be a little more contemporary. That is matter of practice. One must read a lot more. If you pay attention to the kind of poetry that is written these days, you will realize your poetry is responding to these larger changes too. A few places here—'

'How is that? Explain it to me a little.'

The plea is so earnest that it makes Suhrid feel kindlier towards him. A middle-class man with his job on the line, without any chance left of finding recognition as a poet, and yet such irrepressible enthusiasm about improving his writing. This cannot be an easy thing for him. Suhrid takes a sip of his drink and continues.

'Like, for instance, Abanish-da, I would have never used this word for "golden light". This word has a feeling to it that is not in sync with the rest of the poem or with the times. You could have thought of a different word yet kept the meaning intact. On the other hand, check out the line, "*Holding the sun's blood, I wait, unquenched*", how brilliant!'

Even in the darkness cast by the red-blue-yellow lights, Abanish's eyes light up with joy. Without glancing at him, Suhrid continues.

'This expression, "the sun's blood", what an incredible choice of words and image. Even with the sun's blood you find yourself unquenched. This paradox takes the lines to greater heights. Check the rhyme scheme as well, it is perfectly set to metre. *Holding-the-sun's-blood-I-wait-unquenched.* Perfect. So, the rest of the lines cannot match up to the level of this one. Consequently, a discrepancy arises. My observation as a reader is that the full extent of your poetic potential has not been applied here. That you must do, Abanish-da, and you must give it more time. To yourself, to your writing. Time. Time is a must.'

Behind his glasses his eyes seem to shine. Suhrid pretends to not notice. A man who is never praised is perhaps hurt the most by it. Such men are used to derision, but praise is difficult for them to handle. Suhrid understands that Abanish has now become exactly such a person.

'Take your writing more seriously, Abanish-da. As you see, even if you put your life into something here, no one cares. Today payments are delayed, tomorrow who knows what will happen. Don't compromise on your writing for this. And can I tell you something else? Don't mind . . .'

Abanish nods in agreement and Suhrid continues.

'Please cut down on the drinking. I am not asking you to quit. I, too, find people without any addictions incomprehensible. I am asking you to bring it down. For the past few months, you have been drinking too much. This will harm you from inside and out. Think about Ishita-di and your son. Think about them. If you dedicate this time to writing instead . . .'

'My son writes as well, did you know that?'

Abanish's declaration seems far away from Suhrid's last statement. He falls silent in surprise as Abanish goes on.

'He is like me, writes in secret. At night. Has a diary of his own, perhaps makes his friends read it. I have never managed to be his friend, never managed to do anything. Neither could I become suitable for Ishita, nor for him. But I have read his diary in secret. He writes well, you know. He reads your poetry, tries to understand it. Like you just said, his poetry has all this language and rhythm. He is from this time, he gets things, can retain them. Only if there were someone to guide him . . . I could never become his friend. He submits his poems here and there, I know he does. I can also sense the refusals. That is fine. At least he should not break like me, right?'

Suhrid can sense the anchor Abanish is seeking with this declaration, like a poor man sleeping at a railway station begging for a blanket in the cold.

'Why will he break, Abanish-da? If you say he has it in him, then it will happen one day or the other.'

Abanish hails the waiter in the dim light and orders another peg. It's almost eight and raining outside. It wouldn't matter if they get a little late. There would be trouble at home if he returns drunk anyway, so a couple more pegs would hardly make a difference.

'You are avoiding what I said. Please think about it.'

'I know, Suhrid. You want what is best for me. And I know this is not right. Earlier, I would drink when meeting up with friends over the weekends. But now, if I do not drink every evening, I feel awful. Sometimes I drink during the day as well. This is wrong, this cannot go on, I know that. There are frequent fights at home now. Quite naturally! Ours is a regular middle-class neighbourhood, your Ishita-di is quite well-known in the area. When Ishita vents her anger and the boy listens from the next room, it is very humiliating for me. But it is too late now, Suhrid, there is no way back for me.'

'If you understand so much, Abanish-da, then why are you not trying? It is not as if all this has sustained you well either.'

'Suhrid, I have nothing to say in my defence. I usually listen with my head lowered. Ishita rants for a long time, sometimes she shouts. Then she gets tired, shuts the door on my face and goes to sleep. I feel bad. Not because of what she says to me, though.'

'Then?'

'Ishita is a musician. Her voice is her asset, her life. Such people should not shout like that. It strains their voice. When Ishita screams at me, I feel guilty about causing her harm.'

Suhrid does not know how to respond appropriately to this confession. Instead, in this strangely lit space he sees this peculiar man carefully pouring himself another peg. Then Abanish speaks again. 'This reminds me of something. Do you want to hear it?'

There is something about the way he says it, something tugs at Suhrid. He nods at the question. Abanish takes a long swig from his glass and continues to speak.

'This was nearly twenty-five years ago. I was on my way back from Patna. You must have been in school or college then. Anyway, I had just joined this organization as a trainee reporter. This was during the Bihar elections, and they had sent me to prepare a report. I was there for three days. The return train was at night, scheduled to reach Howrah the next morning. Back then, trains were never this crowded. I got into an empty compartment. I could not sleep that night so I stood a little further away from the door, finishing a cigarette.

A young man, probably your age or younger, was standing at the door, his head sticking out in the wind as he held on to the handle. The train was running at full speed. It was clear he was very high. It did not sit well with me, so I warned him once. But he paid no attention. By then, almost his entire body was leaning outside the door, the wind against his face. It was a cold winter night. Perhaps he was hot from the alcohol. I was afraid he would lose balance and fall to his death. When I approached him and warned him again, he turned towards me and hurled a series of abuses at me in chaste Hindi. It was clearly not going to make a difference. As I stood there contemplating if I should call the ticket checker, I recall catching a glimpse of the train approaching a lamp post and the boy's head sticking out in the opposite direction. Before I could pull him to safety, his head smashed against the post, decapitating him. I was right there, it happened in front of my eyes. I was shaking as the rest of the boy's headless torso stumbled in front of me, still quivering, blood spurting out and staining my clothes red. My limbs went totally numb. And then something strange happened. In two vaults, the bloody headless body keeled over and seemed to leap out of the train in two vaults. By then, more passengers rushed to the spot. Someone pulled the chain. However, unable to stand there, I fell unconscious.'

As Suhrid wonders why Abanish would recall such a ghastly story of all things, the latter takes the last sip of the glass and speaks again.

'Today when I look at myself, I am reminded of that headless body, Suhrid. I have been reduced to something alike, in front of Ishita, in front of my son, in front of you and society, again and again. All that remains is a bleeding body. I will endure a little longer, writhing in pain. Then one day, I will take a leap and vanish in the darkness.

Suhrid can sense his voice choking with emotion. He holds Abanish's trembling right hand in his.

'Don't talk like this, please. We are here still, are we not? Tell me.'

Yet again Abanish's answer seems to come from somewhere far away.

'The thing is, Suhrid, I am hiding in that archaic word for "golden light". That is me. Ancient, inadequate, out of use and rejected. An odd one out among the new words, hanging on somehow, sticking out like a sore thumb. I can see this word is harming the rest of the poem, but I cannot remove it. Not all poems are perfect. Let me stay awhile, okay? What do you say?'

Suhrid can sense Abanish's vision going blurry. He knows it's not because of the alcohol.

11

I have always wanted to visit Coffee House on a rainy day like this. I have been there a couple of times before with Abhijit. His college is somewhere nearby and on occasions when I have gone to meet him, he has taken me there. But what happened today was fun in a totally different way. What happened afterwards was even better.

It was clear from around noon that it was going to rain. I had only two classes, so I gathered the courage and bunked them. Moreover, we were supposed to meet at four in front of College Street Coffee House anyway. Nirban sent for us because there was something important to discuss. I suggested we meet at his place, but he would not listen. He had to go to College Street for some books and Soutak's and Simanta's college was nearby so it would be convenient for them. So it was decided we would all meet there. Not a bad plan, especially on a day like this, irrespective of what needed to be discussed. The new edition of the journal was out too and Nirban was supposed to pick it up from Pradip-da's on his way here. A celebration was a must so College Street was chosen as the venue.

I am always so excited whenever I am at College Street Coffee House. I don't know if it's the same with others. Who knows, perhaps our table was once shared by the likes of Shakti Chattopadhyay, Sunil Gangopadhyay, Purnendu Patri, Nabaneeta Dev Sen, Tarapada Roy, Utpal Kumar Basu, Kavita Sinha and Soumitra Chattopadhyay, among many other luminaries. Perhaps at that very table Shakti or Sunil had brought their new pieces to read out for the very first time. Perhaps the reading had taken the place by storm, long before it was to be published and become a legendary work of literature. Just thinking about it sends a shiver down my spine. The pale-yellow walls, the high ceiling with the ancient fans suspended from it, the life-size doors and windows, the entire place has an air of receding into the past, akin to the thrill of stepping into a time machine. Then there is the antique clock above the counter, the one that has seen much time flow by. And it watches over us too!

It began to pour just as we entered Coffee House. Anuroop was yet to reach, Khurshid and Manideepa had come in from the other side and taken a table already. Soutak and Simanta, being engineering students, are always under immense pressure. But they are just as serious about writing—that is something I really like about them. Anuja is very different from the rest of the group. I mean, she barely speaks. We have met on numerous weekends and also worked together on an edition of the journal, but I have hardly heard her utter a word. She is studying to be a doctor and is not interested in writing poetry. Nonetheless, she is a part of the group. Her love for both poetry as well as Anuroop keeps drawing her back to us. Khurshid and Manideepa are students of physics and they, too, have much on their hands with the semester coming up. But I knew no one would be able to ignore Nirban's summons, everyone would turn up.

And everyone did. Some walked in closing their umbrellas, soaked to the bone. But they still came. By then we had ordered infusion and two plates of chicken pakoras—it was the perfect combination to enjoy the rains. A waiter as time-worn as the wall clock itself came and laid out the plates and cups on our table with a grave expression on his face. In almost all restaurants the waiters usually have a sliver of a smile on their faces to please the patrons. It is only in Coffee House that they serve their patrons with the most serious countenance. More than serious, a bit morose actually, as if they literally don't owe anyone a smile. Who knows, perhaps because they spend their entire day in that ancient building they seem so blue.

'Saswata won't be coming?' I began as I bit into a pakora. The white layer of meat at the centre was scalding hot. It was a greedy bite, but I hadn't had one in a while.

'He won't be coming for a few days. His work begins around this time. There isn't much time, just a month and a half left.' Soutak picked up a pakora as he replied. He was drenched, I was afraid he was going to catch a cold.

'What do you mean by that? What work?' I enquired again. Being an introvert, I have not socialized too much with any of the others, except Nirban. Although I like everyone's work, I am especially fond of the three of them. There is no harm in admitting this: Nirban's writings, Khurshid's poems and Saswata's too. The three of them are uniquely different, but I like each of their work a lot. Soutak's answer only made me realize that I did not know much about the group, and it was entirely my fault. Almost reading my thoughts, Nirban replied, 'You probably don't know, Pushkar. Saswata makes idols, it is their family profession—Vishwakarma, Durga, Lakshmi, Kali, all kinds. He himself is a skilled artist. These days, quite a few big Pujo committees place orders for his idols. And that is how he earns his living. There was a time when he had to struggle a lot, but now gradually he has begun to taste success. He is continuing with his studies, wants to get a regular job too. However, he does not wish to give up this profession. Pujo is just a month and a half away, there is a lot of work going on at his place. You will probably find him giving the finishing touches to the straw frames and adding on the first layer of clay. You will like it if you visit him at his studio, we have all been there.'

It was oddly pleasing to hear that. Since I was a child, I have visited Pujo pandals and noticed the names of the artists accompanying the idols. But I have never met an idol-maker in person. When I found out about Saswata, I felt a kind of love and respect for him growing within me. I realized that is why there is a certain flavour of the earth in his writings, a certain kind of simplicity. Making idols is like writing poetry or creating music, isn't it? The latter are the two skills I have observed closely at home growing up, I do not know much about anything else. There is a particular process to creating something—carrying around an idea once it has formed in the head, writing it down, editing it, abandoning it, finally getting it printed and sending it out to the readers in the form of printed words. This is a long road. Take music, for instance, classical music. Picking a raag according to the mood and time, introducing it through the *alaap*, then gradually going into the details—the *sargam*, the *taan*, taking it to the fast-paced bandish and carrying it till the end. There are so many similarities, aren't there? Making an idol is much the same. From the wood and the bamboo to the straw frame, then the clay and the colours, letting it dry before putting on the clothes, the hair and adding the weapons—it is much the same process. All artists have to traverse these long roads. There are no shortcuts.

'This edition has turned out well. There are hardly any errors, I have checked it thoroughly. Here, these are your copies.'

Nirban took out copies of the latest edition and handed them to us. Outside, College Street was beginning to grow hazier. The trees were swinging and swaying in the heavy rains. Inside, the tube lights were coming on one by one. The entire thing seemed incredible to me. This was the first time I was going to see my name in print. It did not matter if anyone got around to reading it, the fact that it had happened was astounding to me. I checked the contents, my poem was on page 137. As I sat deciding whether I was going to take a look at it right there or in the privacy of my own home, Nirban spoke again. 'Now, the reason why I asked all of you to come here today. We are not doing the next edition.'

This was unlike Nirban. 'We won't', 'We can't', these concepts don't exist for him. Neither does he accept such excuses from anyone else. If it is supposed to happen, it will happen. Even if things seem otherwise, it must be done. That is the kind of person he is. So, it was strange to hear him say we were not going ahead with the next issue. Manideepa had just picked up a pakora; she could not even take a bite once she heard him.

'We will not? Why? We had already decided what would go in it. What happened all of a sudden?' she asked. Truly, we had decided everything, whose essays, whose short stories, whose series of poems, whose interviews and so on. We were all staring at Nirban in curiosity when he smiled and said, 'Because instead of an edition we are doing a book. A book of poems.'

It was such a surprising declaration that we all froze for an instant. Meanwhile, Nirban picked up the pakora Manideepa had put down and took a bite of it. 'Why are you all staring at me like that? Can't we bring out a book?'

I was yet to fully grasp what he was saying. Eventually, Khurshid cleared his throat and asked the question that was on everyone's mind. 'But who will publish our book? No one knows us, why would they be interested in our work?'

I looked around at the rest and sensed they were all thinking the same thing. Our own book, who does not want that! At least all of us do. But where would we find a publisher? We are all first-year students, our poems are published mostly in our own journal. Who is going to bring out a book of such poems? The rain was beginning to lighten up outside and the skies were starting to clear, there was a hint of sunlight too.

Nirban went on. 'I think you are all forgetting that *Ebong Shomoy* is a registered publication now. The details arrived from Delhi a few days ago and now we can publish books if we wish to. See, we have been writing together for years now, bringing out this journal. No one knows where each of us will be in the next few years. Some of us might move out of the country for work or we might remain here, nothing is certain. Maybe we will all be here working on this journal for many more years to come, maybe not. I am not saying none of us are ever going to have a book of their own. It will happen. At some point some of us are going to find publishers, get book offers. But what if we have a book of our own before that? A book not just for the sake of it, something to preserve the memories of this time. No matter what happens in the future, we will always have this one book that connects us. Can't we do this?'

We were all still quiet. We could understand what he was saying, but we could scarcely believe it. Nirban glanced at each of us with the same smile on his face and then, with a lot of attitude, summoned the morose waiter from before to order another round of infusion for the table. 'Don't worry, this is on me.'

An extra cup was certainly a matter of concern for some of us because it meant less for the bus fare and consequently getting off midway and having to walk home. However, Nirban has always been generous about such things. Although none of us were thinking of the price of extra infusion at that point. Nirban figured that out and went on.

'I don't get it why all of you are still staring at me, dumfounded like idiots. Seven of us write poetry, isn't it? This will not be like other books of poems. We won't have seven separate books, we will have one book with poems of seven poets. Inside, each person's poems will be arranged like a separate book. For instance, where Manideepa's book ends is where Pushkar's will begin. It will cost less and seven of us will be on the same cover. I have worked it all out. If we have forty pages for each poet, then that is two-hundred-and eighty pages right there, plus another twenty for the cover, the contents, the flyleaves and so on. A single three-hundred-page book of poems belonging to all of us. It will cost more than the journal, so we will have to contribute more this time. Plus I spoke to Pradip-da today. We do not have to pay the whole sum together. Now do you agree?'

Manideepa and Soutak nearly jumped at him, you know, as they drew him into a hug. None of us could have come up with this, honestly. Yet he had thought of everything so easily. That is why he is the editor, our leader. By the time we all agreed and walked out, the rain had stopped. Sunlight was gleaming on the tram tracks while everything around us was soaking wet. We set out for the metro, taking the footpath in front of Presidency College to the shortcut through Medical College further along. Suddenly my eyes fell on the rows of bookshops along the road. For a moment it seemed, and I am not exaggerating one bit, that I had strayed into a different world. A world that was only concerned with books, only listened to books and spoke about books with others. I have been visiting College Street for so long, I have seen so many such shops. I do not have a book to my name, neither did I have ever imagine it would happen. So, I used to feel like an outsider in that world. Today as I was walking down College Street through that glittering sunlight, I felt for the first time that I would finally have a roof over my head in this world. I would have a book of my own among millions of others. Even if no one knows about it, no one reads it or not even a single copy is sold, it would still be there somewhere. And that is how I will remain in this world as well. When at night shopkeepers pull down their shutters and head home, in some shop somewhere, on a shelf among other books,

I will be there with my poems. I will lie in bed and sense that far away, in some neighbourhood, in another world, my book is awake like me. Just as alone as I am . . .

The words trail off in Pushkar's head. He had not been speaking out aloud anyway but now his mind goes quiet as well. It rained here this afternoon, the roads are still wet. The milkwood tree, his friend, is clearly happy with the news of his book, Pushkar can tell. For the first time this year, he can smell its flowers. It's a potent and intoxicating smell.

The flowers are about to bloom.

The month of Aashwin is just around the corner.

So is the book.

12

Most days, Pritha stays back in Ishita's room long after their class is over. It is not as if she lives nearby, but she does not feel like going back home, so strong is the affection that connects her to this tiny music room. A house is, after all, a place where love resides, where one feels like living. The house she knows as her own, her heart does not feel at home there. It has been a few years since her mother's passing, her father passed away recently as well. Nowadays, there is some trouble or the other with her brother and his wife, for various reasons. Getting past all that, beyond the labour and patience of her college job, she can only relax when she reaches Ishita's music room. So, on most evenings, she stays back after class to have a casual chat with Ishita, like she does today.

Ishita prepares a paan for herself, an indulgence going back many years. Placing the betel leaf on one's palm, smearing it with lime, catechu and betel nuts, a dash of strong and fragrant zarda, and then folding it into a triangle before popping it into one's mouth. Pritha has laid the tanpura down but is still strumming it. The Raag Bihag she had been playing was done a little while ago, but she does not feel like stopping. Continuing to caress the strings, she turns to Ishita.

'Didi, can I ask you something? Although it has been a while . . .'

'This is what your problem is, Pritha.' Ishita did not raise her eyes. 'So what if it has been a long time? Even five or ten years is not enough time to perfect a raag. How long have you been learning the Bihag? About four months or so, right? You are not yet prepared to get into the raag. Will it work if you already look for the denouement? These days, all I see is people keeping tally, how many raags they learnt in a year. But music does not happen this way, nothing does. The first thing you need to understand is that if you can succeed in learning the cadence of one raag, it will help you reach the others as well. That is the base, the foundation. Like the Bihag is for you. Its pathways, moods, pace and form, when these things complement each other not just in your voice but in *you*, then you will be able to approach the other raags a lot easily. Forget the others, you must keep learning the Bihag for a long time. Do you know, when Baba managed to get a house on rent in Kolkata, for eight years straight, he used to practise the raag Bhoopali twice a day. Just that, nothing else. All that was pent up in him, it took eight years to get over. Eventually, the house came to be known as Bhoopali House. I'm not asking for eight years, give me one year, set that time aside for Bihag.'

Pritha knows the fault is hers. This happens with her at home and in the college staff room as well because of the way she speaks. She gets uneasy and does not finish: lets her words float midway, expecting the other person to understand. It does not work out all the time, like it did not work out now.

'No, Didi, that is not what I meant at all. If you want, you can teach me Bihag all my life, I am in no hurry. How many have the good fortune of learning one raag properly?'

'Great! I would have been disappointed if you were in a hurry. Then what were you saying?' Ishita asks, a little relieved.

'Well, although it has been a while since the incident, there still is a question on my mind. There is no doubt that you were correct in turning down Mr Haldar's offer the other day. Why must an artist like you sit for an exam? Why do you have to prove yourself? You were right in what you did. But I was thinking, you are part of such an illustrious gharana. The daughter of such a father. Yet you have no recordings of your own. You should have some, Didi! So that everyone gets to hear your voice. Not just one, but multiple cassettes. So, I was wondering, instead of downright turning him down like that, is there another way to make your recording happen? This has been bothering me since then.'

Ishita raises her head at the question. She lightly sets down the betel leaf and the container of catechu on top of the box.

'Baba came to Kolkata from Faridpur during Partition. Walked to this country with all his things packed in one trunk. He was newly married. Ma was back home in the old country. He had given her his word that he was going to find a job and provide a roof over their heads as soon as possible. That he would bring her here as soon as he succeeded. Because it was a tumultuous time back then, one was never sure what would happen next and where. Well, though he turned up in Kolkata, there was nothing he could do except sing. It was only music that was on his mind; in fact, it was one of the reasons why he came here. Kolkata of those days was famous for its artists and *ustaad*s. All he wished was to have someone like them as his guru. But all that was for later. At first, he had to figure out food and sustenance. During the days he would work as a load bearer for less than minimum wage. He would then spend the nights on the footpaths of Sealdah, resting his head on bricks. Later, he managed to find a quiet porch of a house where he started taking shelter at night. One night, he woke up to the feeling of a police baton poking him. The police informed him he could not sleep there, since it was illegal. Baba tried explaining to them with folded hands that he had nowhere else to go. How could he function without a good night's sleep after all the hard work? But the police officer was adamant. He enquired as to what Baba did for a living. For some reason, Baba blurted out, "I sing." Immediately, the officer ordered, "Sing for me right now." Kolkata was a strange city back then. Today, you cannot imagine this scene unfolding anywhere at midnight. Baba sung a Bhairavi thumri for the man, *'Jamuna ke teer'*. Ustad Abdul Karim Khan saab was Baba's idol, so he sang a thumri in that fashion. After he finished the song, he opened his eyes to find the officer, having dropped his baton on the ground, weeping helplessly. He gave Baba his word that as long as he patrolled that area, no one would bother him. The officer, however, had one request. He would come back from time to time to hear him sing. That was how it began for Baba in Kolkata. A place to sleep in exchange for Raag Bhairavi. He went on to earn great renown across the country as a singer, with lakhs of admirers who would surround him at all times. He even built his own three-storey house in south Kolkata, named it after the raag he created. Isn't it a fairy-tale life?'

Pritha realizes that her slender fingers had unwittingly stopped on the strings of the tanpura, like how trams abruptly halt on their tracks. She comes to with a start as if it was indeed a tale she was hearing. 'Even in fairy tales there aren't such highs and lows.'

'True, only life has the audacity to do that.' Ishita turns to look out the window. Then she turns back her gaze and continues.

'But that's not why I began telling the story about Baba. He who managed to carve out his own space among people after so many struggles, towards the end of his life was conferred a Padma Shri. By then he was ailing, he could not perform any more and mostly stayed at home. He passed away two years later. When the letter with the news of the Padma Shri arrived, he spent the entire day sitting quietly beside the window wrapped in a white blanket. Then, in the afternoon, when one of his students came, he made the boy type out a letter on his pad. A letter of refusal. Both Dada and I were in the room at that time. We could understand from the look on his face how hurt he was. Even artists of the next generation had been conferred that award by then. It was too little, too late. In his letter Baba clearly stated the reason for his refusal. We could understand why. Compared to an entire life's worth of struggles and dedication, no honour, not even a Padma Shri, amounted to anything. That night when I took his dinner to his room, I did not say a word. As I was stepping out, I suddenly heard him speak from behind. "The thing is, I have never approached anyone with palms extended asking for any honour. So today I cannot compliantly accept dishonour either." That day, that night, that single sentence changed my life and my point of view. If Baba had accepted the Padma Shri that day, I would have probably gone for that audition today. The fact that I could not is because of that day. Such a man my father was. Today, if I sit for this audition, it will belittle his legacy as well. I cannot allow that.'

Pritha is silent.

Ishita is silent.

The tanpura is silent.

The Bihag is silent.

Flecks of catechu dots fall on the betel leaf.

The leaf turns red. Like blood.

The blood of an entire life's efforts.

Like the blood staining Abanish's temple as he surreptitiously avoids the music room while trying to stumble to the other door along the veranda that leads inside. Today the fracas in the office had gone up, so he had borrowed two hundred rupees from Hitanshu and left work early. After getting roaring drunk, when he got off the bus at the crossing of the locality, he could barely stand on his feet. He did not have lunch today so getting drunk on an empty stomach made him lose all control of himself. He was still trying to figure his way back home when he stumbled and fell on a rock while trying to skirt a cycle around the corner. Abanish knows if Ishita finds him like this, she will fly into a fit of rage and he will never hear the end of it. It will only stress her voice, hamper her singing. Wanting to avoid that situation, Abanish tries to get to the tiny room on the other side. His son's room, which remains closed when he is not there, just as it is now. There is cotton and Dettol in there. All he needs to do is stop the bleeding somehow and go to bed. If asked, he can always say he had had dinner outside.

These days he does not get to come to his son's room. The fact that he gets to come home at all is strange, he wonders. There are so few things in this room that even with unsteady feet he does not find it difficult to locate the switch of the table lamp. The medicine box should be there somewhere, he just needs to look for it. In the low light Abanish comes to an abrupt halt. There is a sheaf of ruled full-scape paper lying on the desk, carefully kept, neatly arranged. The first page is blank, but as he turns it over, he finds pages and pages of poems inside. A manuscript. A first manuscript. His son's.

At once Abanish notices how much his son's handwriting has come to resemble his own. Is his poetry similar too? He tries to read, but his vision is too blurry. Despite that, he picks up the second page and begins to read.

Can you last just two more windy days, Banani?
As you overcome these unwelcome lodgings,
Summon in you the patience of a bird in the dark.

In the morning you will see, far away, at the turn of the tiny river

A bursting marine life, horse hoof shaped
And a boat tied somewhere or the other.

Your sleepless eyes now seek rest from the cold wind,
But the memories keep you awake
Its waves making you forget.

Just two more days. Surely then a bridge to another planet
Will appear on this earthly paddy field bathed in divine
light
And at once two worldly people will be born, I know.

My heart is four years older than yours
I am an expert diver, and I bet the seven seas
Close your eyes and wait, hold on to courage—

We will live, you will see, tomorrow, or even today!

Beneath the low light, the ruled paper trembles as Abanish
keeps staring at it for the longest time. How much Pushkar's
poetry has changed, how different it is from his. Not that it
had to be alike. Times are different, people are different, the
language, the thoughts, everything is different. Father and
son. Two entirely different individuals, connected only by
blood. It takes Abanish quite a bit of time just to figure out
that there is no similarity in thought or language between his
poetry and Pushkar's. His son's poetry has somehow taken a
route quite distant from his, just as his son has grown distant
from him without him realizing it. Have they grown distant or
has more distance crept between them in its floating, invisible
form? The poetry is bound to be different. Language is all
about people. It is through language that a person becomes

different from another. Languages change from one body to another, from one soul to another. Abanish keeps staring at a stranger's language as he sways and floats in that space.

The thought makes him feel good. Their poetry is diverging—their paths, their lives as well. Absolutely stealthily. Exhausted and unable to stand on his feet any longer, Abanish plops down in a chair in front of the desk. He cannot remember why he had come to his son's room in the first place. All he can remember is a documentary he had watched on television. The autobiography of a space shuttle. How it travels and goes miles and miles outside the earth's atmosphere into the black depths of space, with its huge mechanical body. Once there, how its body begins to separate into fragments, only a small component is of use there. The two other bigger parts are merely accompaniments, meant to help the smaller part get there. Abanish remembers watching the two parts uncoupling and separating, freeing the smaller part to float in the vast unknown of space. Then the three parts begin to drift apart in different directions. Perhaps they never meet again, reflects Abanish.

How far have they come then, in space? Have they reached that point in time? When you must uncouple, detach yourself and separate? Like language, like ideas, like poetry? As he tries to stand up, Abanish realizes he no longer has any connection with the floor. He has no connection with anything. Everything seems to float around him, defying gravity. Everything is up in the air, including him. Only the blood, the blood has stopped flowing.

13

'Come in, come in. How are you? Come inside.'

The smile that lights up Gunjan sir's face on seeing him is a genuine one; it takes Pushkar no time to figure that out. The man cannot force a smile, something even his students know. Such a sociable, gracious and understanding person and a good teacher too, how can one not love such a person? That is why Pushkar pays this smiling, middle-aged man a visit from time to time, to make sense of things, without ever being turned down, though he is not Gunjan sir's student.

Today he has come looking for solutions to two of his problems and the fact that he will go back with an answer makes him feel lighter and better already. Although for that, Pushkar will have to share with Gunjan sir one of his deepest secrets, something he had never thought he would do voluntarily. But Gunjan sir is like a doctor, one should hide nothing from him.

'Tell me, Pushkar, where are you stuck?'

Seating him on one side of one of the empty, long tables, Gunjan sir asks him the question while lighting up a cigarette by the window. The evening batch had left some time ago. With some amount of trepidation, Pushkar pulls out a heavy book from his bag and places it on the table. The problem with the book, as per Pushkar, is that more than its physical weight, the ideas conveyed in it and the language seem a lot heavier. That is why he has been unable to make much headway with it. Neither has he been able to return it to Nirban. Hence his turning up at Gunjan sir's door.

Blowing smoke out the window, Gunjan sir turns his gaze towards the book.

'What! *Remembrance of Things Past*? Suddenly? Who gave you this? Or did you have a copy at home?'

'No, Sir, not mine. This belongs to a friend.'

'Your friend gave this to you to read? Interesting!'

'Actually, he reads a lot. Literature from various countries. He runs a journal of his own, writes too. He was the one who asked me to read this.'

'Hmm. Are you reading it then?'

'I am here to see you because I am finding it difficult. I am stuck, I have not been able to get past the third chapter. The writing seems a little different. And the language too. I was wondering if you could help me.'

Gunjan sir smiles at him, stubs out the half-smoked cigarette in the ashtray and pulls out a chair opposite Pushkar at the table.

'See, Pushkar. Explaining the essence of this book to you is something I cannot possibly do. Even I am trying to understand it, well, *trying to*. Since I picked up the book a while ago, I have managed to get a little ahead of you, but that's about it. To be honest, in every language of the world perhaps there are a couple of texts like this, which cannot be explained in clear terms. Perhaps one can try and make sense of them in one's own terms, but they are quite difficult to explain to someone else. I believe this book by Proust is one such text. It is you who must explore its depths, no one else can take you on that journey. Have you ever seen a mine? You are a geography student, you must have geology as a subject as well. The minerals you study about, have you ever seen their mines? Any mine, for that matter?'

'No, I haven't.'

'You will perhaps someday. You cannot suddenly dig a huge hole. At first a few people have to venture inside to ascertain if indeed it holds coal, gold, oil or some such deposit. Only then does mining begin. Isn't that right?'

'Yes, Sir.'

'Yes, so that first entry into the mine happens through a narrow tunnel. Not always, but often. First the machines are lowered, and then one by one people go down to check the area out. Imagine this book is one such mine, a mine whose excavation is not yet finished. Forget many people, even two people together cannot brave its depth. One must do it alone. You must do so too. By yourself.'

As the weight of the words settle on him, Pushkar cannot help but feel a little sad. Will he ever be able to truly understand the complexity of such a book? All by himself? He wonders if dejection is reflected on his face.

Gunjan sir continues, 'But let me tell you, Pushkar, one needs a lot of preparation to approach this book. You must have read the literature of various countries, but it will serve you best if you start reading this book later. One must traverse quite a few steps before reaching this book, so if you don't go through those steps, then this book will seem even more incomprehensible. For example, let us say you have begun reading Bengali literature. Now if the third or fourth book you read is a Kamal Kumar or a Satinath Bhaduri, then you will hit a roadblock, because in order to understand them, you have to first understand a number of other people. Marcel Proust is like that, this book is like that. Let me tell you something, Pushkar. It is somewhat funny. Memory. What is the first thing that comes to your mind when you hear this word?'

'The past,' Pushkar replies without much thought.

'Correct! That's what everyone thinks. The past. However, if you think of it vis-à-vis time, memory is never a thing of the past. It is in the present, as well as the future.' Sensing that this has not made much sense to Pushkar, Gunjan sir goes on to explain. 'When a particular incident is in your memory, even if it is a past incident, you are nurturing the memory in the present. It was not a memory for you in the past, it has become a memory *now*. Here you are sitting in front of me. Is this part of your memory? It isn't, right? But this evening will be a memory for you in the future. Two or ten years later, one day if you recall this evening, then this memory will be kindled. As in, the memory will come to life at that point. Right? Therefore, every moment of the present is raw material to produce memories for the future. Moreover, what do the memories themselves contain? A fragment of the past. Something that was once your present but will never be your future.'

Pushkar cannot claim the entire thing is clear to him now, but he still nods in agreement. Gunjan sir laughs.

'See, this memory business is very challenging. I know I have probably not been able to explain anything. But one thing you must be aware of, a book that was written with something this difficult as its central idea must hold complexity as its primary condition of study. A book like this cannot be read so easily. Or perhaps it can never be read fully. One just has to try, that's it.'

Pushkar can tell he has come to the right person. Who else would have spent so much time explaining all this to him? But he begins to feel a little hesitant as approaches the second problem because for that, he must share that secret of his with Gunjan sir.

'Sir, there was something else.'

'Tell me, this time is yours. Tell me.'

His words are so reassuring that they give Pushkar a boost of courage.

'Sir, I dabble in poetry, have been for a couple of years now.'

Gunjan sir leaps up from his chair at these words and claps him on the back excitedly.

'What! Why haven't you told me before? Excellent!'

As Pushkar attempts to get up out of discomfort and embarrassment, Gunjan sir claps him on the shoulder once again to make him sit down before returning to his chair.

'This reveal has made me very happy, Pushkar. Nothing can be better than this. I keep hearing around me that kids these days do not read literature, let alone write any. You are a living, breathing example to the contrary. Very good, keep it up. Do bring by some of your work for me to read.'

His words stoke Pushkar's embarrassment further, but he manages to rein himself in.

'Sir, that is what I had a question about.'

'Of course, what is it?'

'Actually, the boy who lent me this book, Nirban, him and some of us are bringing out a book. A collection of our own poems.'

'That is great news! I will buy a copy. Keep one for me.'

'Sir, I will give you a copy anyway. The problem lies elsewhere.'

'What is it?'

'I have been writing since I was a child . . . just poetry. You are the first person I am telling this. A few diaries have piled up on my desk. I have compiled a manuscript of things I have written over the last three years. It was done in a bit of a haste because it needs to be submitted to the printer day after. But now that I am reading the poems, they don't sound like they did earlier. I don't feel confident about them. It is as if I am unable to find my way back. As if I am unable to express myself. All the pieces seem incomplete now although when I was writing them, they didn't feel so. The trouble is, does it make sense keeping these pieces in the manuscript? I am not asking you to read the poems, just tell me what I should do at this point. I cannot seem to find a way.'

Another reassuring smile brightens up Gunjan sir's face. He lights a cigarette and goes to stand by the window again. Pushkar can only wait silently, hoping for an answer, as Gunjan sir blows puffs of smoke out the window while gazing into the distance.

'If you are serious about writing, Pushkar, then this question, this discomfort will haunt you for the rest of your life. This does not become apparent while writing: at that time an emotion, a determination drives one forward. That's the case with everyone. However, when you look at it afterwards from a distance, this dissatisfaction, this feeling of inadequacy, this pain of something missing somewhere, you will not be able to escape it your entire life. No matter how much you write, how big you become. In fact, even if your writing is celebrated one day, sitting at your own table, you will rediscover this frustration time and again. The day you stop experiencing this feeling any more, you can be sure that's the day your writing meets its demise. It feels good to see this doubt, this hesitation in you. And because you possess this, you must keep creating, you must not stop.

'Let me tell you a short story. I cannot seem to remember if it's a story or a real incident. You know how with time it is difficult to tell the difference between the two. Proust wrote, "Remembrance of things past is not necessarily the remembrance of things as they were." As in, whatever happened in the past, it is not as if memories reflect those events exactly. We often tend to recall things differently. Sometimes memories are also created by mixing reality with a dash of imagination. Some incidents you perhaps hoped would turn a certain way but they didn't. Memories can morph the incident a little and represent it in a slightly distorted manner, unable to turn down the commands of your expectation. There is nothing wrong with it. They are your memories, your desires, after all. That is when stories and incidents become indistinguishable. Anyway, once upon a time, in some port city in the West, a misty haze covered the land most of the time. The fumes of huge ships docking at the port every day and the awful pollution emitted from the factories combined with the local weather to create this situation. It was not really a very big city, perhaps a settlement of about two hundred homes, but it was always shrouded in this thick smog. At times, things would get so bad that it became impossible to see anything beyond a few metres. This was year-round. In that port city there lived an old man who used to deliver letters and packages from door to door, braving this smog. While the rest of the people would go out in groups with torches trying to find their way around, this old man, with his unerringly accurate calculation, could go from house to house all by himself. He would even show tourists around when the fog was the thickest. One day, both the port and the factory shut down and the pollution receded, significantly improving the weather. Sunlight cut through the haze and flooded the little city with its brightness. Everyone was jubilant, finally they could move about freely. Only the old man was devastated. Because he could no longer recognize anything—the roads, the markets, the houses, everything was unrecognizable to him suddenly. It was the smog that used to show him the way. He was so miserable that it was not long before he passed away. Poetry is much like that little port city. And you are that old man. As long as there is doubt, hesitation, discontent, there will be a fog. And you will be able to make your way through it. The day all this goes away, everything clears up and the sunlight floods in, you will not be able to recognize anything. Poetry, too, will cease to exist. So, it is through this haze that you must walk, write and develop your manuscript. For you have chosen this miasma yourself. That is poetry.'

Pushkar closes his eyes and tries to visualize the fog engulfing the tiny city. He envisions his manuscript, his forthcoming book. It is evident that coming to see Gunjan sir was a wise decision. As he rises to leave, taking advantage of Sir's distraction to touch his feet, the latter turns to him and wraps him in a tight hug. The kind of hug Pushkar is not used to. For an instant his nose traces the collar of Sir's shirt smelling of cigarette smoke, then the moment is gone and Pushkar turns towards the door. As he is about to go down the staircase, Gunjan sir, having followed him till the mouth of the staircase, calls out to him. 'Let me tell you something, Pushkar. I'm saying this because it's you, because you will understand. You told me a couple of times you are writing poetry. You did, didn't you? Never speak like that again if you can.'

Realizing that Pushkar is a little dumbstruck by this request Gunjan sir continues.

'Actually, there is something specific when you say "writing". Isn't it so? There is a sense of reaching a goal, a sense of achievement, right? You did not use the term thinking all of this, but the moment you say, "I am writing poetry", that very moment what you are implying is a sense of finality to it, something you are completing. But that never happens. Not just for poetry, it does not happen for any work of art. No one can say with any kind of certainty that they have finished a painting or made a film or sung a song. That is because there is something intangible in all forms of art, something one cannot reach, one cannot touch, no matter how renowned the artist. Because art, like space, is an infinite medium, it has expanse but no limits, it exists but is mostly uncharted. No matter how deep you venture, it will never be possible for you to completely attain it. It will never be possible to reach its centre. No one has ever managed to do that. What you can do your entire life is make a desperate attempt to attain that centre, take a daring plunge to trace its depth. Some go only a small way, some succeed in going a little further and only a few manage to go very far. It all depends on a person's talent, although no one will be able to complete the journey. That is because you can perceive art, but you can never truly touch it. So, what you can say or think instead is that you are just *trying* to write poems. Because you really are doing that, every day. If you say you are writing poems, that evokes a sense of fullness, a sense of accomplishment which is completely false. You will come across many such people around you, those who are very confident about themselves and their art, and those who are convinced they have made it to the centre. There will be many like those. Why must you become like them? Rather, there is a lot more honesty, a greater kind of truth, in continuing to try. It is the best course of action. The truth is that a work of art can be effective, but it is not always successful. Most are unable to distinguish between the two. You must keep this difference in mind, alright? And never stop trying. Will you keep this in mind?'

'Yes, I shall. Thank you, Sir.'

Pushkar walks out of the house bidding Gunjan sir goodbye and takes the road by the lake, walking quietly and unmindfully, Sir's final words echoing in his head. Try, try. Set oneself afloat or keep running, despite knowing you will never reach there. What a strange addiction this is, what a weird kind of stupor. Pushkar looks up at the evening sky, the clouds have dissipated by now. There is a single star high above, its light twinkling, clearly visible. But it can never be touched and Pushkar knows it too.

14

Saheli,

*Your letter sparked such a surge of affection that it has taken me
a while to reply. I deliberately did not call you in the meanwhile,
because I could hear your voice again and again while reading
the letter. Such a beautifully written letter. Exactly how you talk.
That is not an easy thing to accomplish because most people tend
to shift to a different kind of language while writing, a language
not their own. That is easier to do. To bring across the way you
speak and transfer it to writing is much more difficult. I am not
patronizing you; this is really how I feel about it. I regret that all
these years I have only made you read my inane words but never
once attempted to listen to yours. But when I read your letter, it
became clear to me that you must be writing something or the
other in secret too. Much more clandestinely than me, or I would
have at least known.*

*That day when you came to college, I never thought the visit
would culminate in a letter, that too such a letter. Once I read it,
I realized I have never managed to hide from you the part of me*

that I wished to hide and neither did you wish to conceal the fact that you knew. How beautifully these opposites come together in your letter. I cannot explain to you how easy you have made my days and nights.

I have understood what you have written in the letter, exactly the way you have wanted me to. I would not have, if my feelings had been too different from yours. But believe me, since the day I realized that a significant part of me is irrevocably tied to you, that you have begun to occupy a substantial part of my soul, my thoughts and my writings, even that day I did not assume that this presence of yours has to ever extend to my life. Let me tell you why. You spoke about a ship and the sea. I will tell you about the sea as well. About the first time I saw the sea.

Your parents have taken you to the seaside many times, I know. You have shown me pictures. Goa, Kerala, then Vizag just the other day. Stunning places. Even if we wished to, we did not have the means. Truth be told, perhaps we did not even wish to. I did not see it then, but now I understand when I see my parents, that their desires are no longer alive. All except mine. I am their mutual hope, walking around in the flesh in front of them. Nothing else remains. Whatever, let's not dwell on it. Besides, my parents did not have the means to take us on a yearly vacation. Sometimes a visit to the circus with Baba in the winter or to Gariahat in the summer with Ma, those are the trips I remember taking. So, till Class VII I did not know what the sea looked like. I had seen photos, obviously, but one cannot comprehend the sea through images, so neither did I.

I finally saw the sea when my parents took me to Digha after my Class VII exams. That too, it was not just the three of us, there was one of Ma's cousins who had joined us with his family as well as one of Baba's friends and his daughter. We packed up into two Ambassadors and drove to Digha. It was the usual trip, finding a cheap hotel, getting by on passable rice-dal-fish curry meals twice a day—nothing special. But when I visited the beach, I was stunned to see so much water just floating in front of me. I had heard it was big. But so big! Absolutely endless? Like something without a horizon? When one stands in front of something too beautiful, it's often possible to feel a flicker of fear. I don't know if it happens with you, but it happens with me. The surprising thing is that when you stand in front of something that beautiful, that immense, you also begin to enjoy that feeling of fear.

Everyone went into the sea to bathe, except me. Baba has always been a good swimmer, he swam out really far. In those three days, even Ma waded into waist-deep water. Baba's friend's daughter, barely five years old, even she was carried in. Everyone except me because just before the trip I had been running a temperature and was ill for a week. Since no one was brave enough to take me with them, I used to sit on the beach and watch them. I was especially sad and envious on the first day when I could not step into the water. But from the next day, it stopped bothering me. Because it dawned on me that it was so satisfying to just sit before this expansive, rolling and bottomless mass of water that it was foolish to keep account of whether or not I got to bathe in the sea. Rather, I felt that doing so would be a slight to both the sea's enormity and my immense fascination with it. So, from the very next day, all my envy and sorrow vanished, leaving behind just the astonishment and wonder. That I was finally in front of this massive body of water, that I was witnessing this colossal entity. Could I have hoped for anything more than this concurrence?

I was happy because there was nothing to expect from the sea. What can one expect when faced with something that vast? It is in those depths that all hopes rise and then go under. There is no greater expectation, no greater desire. The sea was right in front of me, I stood before it, what else could I want?

But you know the day before we were supposed to get back, I also got really depressed. We were set to leave early next morning. On our last night, there I was walking back from the beach to the hotel and I remember looking back numerous times. The sea spread out under the light-blue and purple sky, the unbroken sound of breaking waves, twinkling yellow lights of fishing trawlers far out at sea and the heavy, salty air all around. I felt sad removing myself from the presence of that immensity. That feeling lingered even after coming back to Kolkata. Then I told myself, 'I got to witness the sea, wasn't that enough?' There are people who never get to experience that, who do not get the chance to go and stand quietly by the sea. At least I had managed to see it with my own eyes.

I am writing so much for one single reason. To me, love is like that first visit to the sea. I am not getting into which one of us is a ship and which one is a boat. What I do know is that from the day I fell in love with you, from the day that realization set in, within myself I have heard the sound of waves breaking on the seashore and felt the movement of the heavy, salty air. I have recognized that I have no existence in the face of its limitlessness. There is only wonder and astonishment.

Had I not seen the sea, I would have been sad reading your letter. Because then falling in love with you would also mean hoping to possess you. To possess you in the manner everyone assumes is the sole outcome of love. That I will spend my life with you, you know, the kind of thing one easily desires when in love. And perhaps it is quite natural too. But I have laid my eyes on the sea once, I hope or desire for nothing. I do not feel the compulsion to wade into the shallows and take a dip. Because I have been able to love you, been able to give away a big part of myself to you, this feeling has a sense of incalculability against which mortal hopes and desires are too insignificant.

So, your letter has freed me from the burden that you will misunderstand me in some way. Although I should have known that you have seen the sea in much the same manner as I, which is why you could write such a letter. You are right. This is how we will remain. With this invisible mass of water between us whose extent we have no idea about. We will not meet every day, perhaps we will not even talk for long stretches of time, but no matter where we are, we will always be aware of the sea that flows between us. If we read these letters twenty years later, will they sound too romantic? Too made-up? Too sickly poetic? Perhaps they will. But at this moment, this is the truth. So, there is nothing else for me to do at this point than write this letter to you.

Yes, from time to time we must turn back from the sea and return to our lives. We will be sad reminiscing about the lights of the trawlers, the breaking waves and the saline air. But that sadness, too, will become a part of what we like, isn't it? You have made me feel so much lighter, so relieved, do you know? I don't know if we could have talked like this if it were someone else. Nor do I know if I would have been able to love someone this much. Plus that frisson of fear, that unknown dread of being in the presence of something colossal, I felt it the day you first held my hand. And I realized it was not the fear of losing you, but the fear of possessing.

Take care of yourself. If you wish to reply to this letter, don't delay it. And yes, I have not told you yet, there is another reason for my late reply. I have a book coming out. A book of poems. If you hadn't read pages and pages of my writings, hadn't given me the courage to continue, I would have never been able to make this manuscript, let alone think about turning it into a book. That this is happening, you have a major role in it.

Would you like to come see the sea with me some day? Some day?

Pushkar

While Pushkar is seated at his small writing table folding this letter, at that exact moment, a little far from his house, in the middle of a busy road, another pair of hands is repeatedly folding another piece of paper. Unfolding, folding again. Automatically, without wanting to, unconsciously. Like how wind-up toys keep running, long after children have fallen asleep, a useless exercise without any witnesses. Asmita keeps fiddling with the paper in such a manner, standing in the shallow darkness in one corner of the 8B bus terminus. All around her is a steady stream of busy indifference, completely ignoring her. The fact that she has chosen this slightly dark spot is perhaps more to hide her existence from herself. It is incredibly difficult to avoid one's own self, in these past few days she has realized how much. Asmita had opened the note Pushkar had delivered to her, thinking it was a proper letter, but found only two lines from Abhijit. 'Meet me once if you can, 7 p.m. tomorrow, 8B bus stand. I will never ask you to meet me again.' No matter what Pushkar had intended to achieve by making Abhijit write the letter, he could have scarcely known the effect would be quite on the contrary.

Since her father caught them by the lake that evening, things have been even more fraught with tension at home. Her father has not been letting her go out alone after college. In the meanwhile, the groom's family had come over to discuss things. She had clenched her teeth and somehow got through the day, like walking on a bed of nails with your eyes shut. Let there be wounds, just avoid seeing the blood. The surveillance on her has been bolstered after that. Nowadays, if she must go out in the evening, she has to take her elder sister along. Asmita does not understand where her sister's allegiance lies. She listens to her as well as her parents and expresses no opinions to either. Maybe she is trying to get through this time too. Today they made up an excuse of some casual wedding shopping. Her didi has gone to the other side to the shop selling stoles so they have something with them when they get back. And then all at once, in the darkness of the bus stop, she finds Abhijit standing right in front of her.

'You had nothing else to say? Just those two lines?'

'Even if I did, what would I have gained from it?'

'Still thinking about gains then?'

'Who knows, someone else could have made losses. It is better to not say anything.'

'Then tell me, why did you ask me to come? I can't stay for long, Didi will be here.'

'You probably think I don't get where you are coming from. In fact, you must think so. I can sense it in the resentment in your voice. But it's not true. I know there is nothing you can do at your end. You would if you could. Despite Pushkar urging me, I did not want to write a letter that was going to make you feel worse. I know it's difficult to get past family pressure. If I were in your place, I would have probably done the same. Neither can I tell you to wait for five more years. Your parents will not support that. I wanted to meet you just so I can tell you this. I have not misunderstood you, I never will. Try and do the same for me, too, if you can.'

'You will never meet me again?'

Her voice trembles at the question. He wishes he had not heard it, for the sake of his own sanity. Their story had begun in a bus stop. Today, when it's ending, they are both back where they had begun. Except the fact that their surroundings are barely recognizable.

Without answering her question, Abhijit hands her a brown envelope.

'I got this for you. I'll get going now. Take care of yourself.'

Without letting her say anything else, Abhijit steps out of the shadow and vanishes in the crowded light. Asmita remains standing there for a while until her sister comes and takes her home in a rickshaw in absolute silence.

Back home, Asmita opens the brown envelope to find a book inside. *Aj Jodi Amay Jigyesh Koro* (If You Ask Me Today). She was never much into poetry. However, in school she had heard many friends talk about Joy Goswami. There would always be two or three of his books in Pushkar's bag and Abhijit reads his poetry as well. He has sent her letters with quotes of the poet in them. Today for the first time, and possibly the last, Abhijit has given her a book written by the poet. Asmita opens to the blank page at the beginning and finds he has written nothing on it, no name, dedication or dates. Absent-mindedly flipping through the pages, she comes across a feather, white and tiny, stuck with gum below the poem printed on page twenty-two of the book.

-    'If they push you into the fire to die?'
     I will die completely sans effort

-    'If they raise you to the clouds?'
     I will fall and shatter with the rain

-    'If they crush you into dust?'
     I will scatter from path to path

-    'Fly? And if they tear up your wings?'
     I will hang on to their branches as I fall

-    'If they shake you off their branches?'
     All I can do is cling to them even more

-    Tell me, O Court, what more is there to say?
     'Go and suffer until the end of your days!'

Asmita sits quietly for some time, with the book spread open on her bed. Then she shuts it and sets it aside. All that is left behind between the covers is the poem, the feather and the remnants of her previous life.

15

Time feels static in the harsh sunlight of the afternoon. It still exists, but it appears frozen to Gunjan. Because he cannot get through to his daughter's phone. Until a little while ago he could not remember what he was doing or how he ended up beside this highway. Not that he can recall much now. It is a wide road that curves like the crescent moon before disappearing in the distance. The sun is beating down, like it happens during the summer in this part of the world. It was beneath that scalding sun on one side of the highway that he found himself a while ago. Is this a suburb of Kolkata or somewhere else, it is difficult to tell. As far as the eye can see, there are no milestones or hoardings. In fact, he has not seen a single car plying on this road all this while. So, he cannot tell for sure where he is. When things like this happen, it gets very disconcerting, exactly how Gunjan feels now.

He still has his college bag on his back, with his books and papers inside. Walking along the highway he suddenly notices a telephone booth up ahead. A wooden frame, glass all around. Transparent, easy to peer inside. It's a usual structure—there's a wooden pedestal with a directory, a box-like metal phone with a receiver hanging from the cradle on one side, square buttons for dialling and a small slot beside it for the coins.

Gunjan glances at his watch, it's three-thirty. It's when he calls his daughter. If he is in college, he usually calls from the teachers' room. This is the time when his daughter returns home from school to the quarters in Bengaluru where she lives with her mother. She is usually alone at this time or with the domestic help, as her mother is at work at this time. Gunjan calls almost every day. Despite being unsure of how he ended up here, he's relieved to find a phone booth. At least he will be able to make the call to his daughter.

A monotonous howling of the wind can be heard, relentless like the sun. As he steps inside the booth and shuts the door behind him, the sounds are instantly drowned out. He fishes inside his pockets and takes out a few one-rupee coins. Putting the first one into the slot, he dials the number as soon as the jingling sound of the coin is heard. However, there is absolute silence at the other end. Usually it rings, or there is a tone to signal that the line is busy. But now there is no sound. This should not be happening. Besides, the machine seems fine. He disconnects the line and dials the number again. Then again. Every time it's the same silence on the other side. Something is wrong somewhere, he is certain.

There is only one coin left. He decides to try a fourth and final time. As he pushes the coin into the slot, he halts abruptly at the sounds it emits. In the anticipation of talking to his daughter he did not notice the sound before—it is not the usual metallic sound coins make when put into slots. He cannot tell exactly how it is different, he just knows it is. This call, too, is met with silence. Gunjan glances outside, the landscape is deserted under the scorching sun. It is still a little comfortable inside the booth.

As he is about to step out, his eyes dart to the floor near his feet. There is a ring embedded in the wooden plank on the floor of the booth. It's unlike anything he has ever seen before. There is nothing to do now, nor is he sure how to get back home from here. So, giving in to his curiosity, he bends over and pulls the ring. With one pull a square portion of the plank comes up, to reveal, much to his surprise, a flight of wooden stairs leading way down below.

The old stairs creak beneath his feet as Gunjan cautiously begins to descend, until after quite a bit, he realizes that it's evening down here. Is time flowing in a line here from top to bottom? Looking around him, he comes to the realization that he has reached a graveyard. All around him he can hear the rustling of dried leaves in whatever little wind that is blowing. There are no trees in sight, nothing discernible above him either. The only thing for certain is that this dying light must be the dusk.

He walks ahead and comes upon four ancient graves set in a row. At the very end, a little further apart, is a brand-new coffin. It looks as if it has been placed there in the last couple of days. He also notices a shining one-rupee coin beside each grave. Is that why he could not get through to her on the phone? He picks up the four coins and puts them back in his pocket. As he walks, the only sound that can be heard is that of his own feet on the rustling leaves. He reads the markings on all four graves as much as can be made out in the dim light. There are four names engraved in English one after another: Tennyson, Wordsworth, Yeats and Baudelaire. Full names, dates of birth and death, everything is etched on the stones. How have these four been laid to rest here side by side? None of it makes sense to him.

He rubs the dirt off the markings; no, it's correct. It is them. The evening has begun to darken in the graveyard. What is in that shiny coffin in the distance? Unable to stymie his curiosity, he walks up to it. There is not much dirt or leaves on this one. He pulls the lid to find layers and layers of frocks and dresses and sweaters, one on top of the other, carelessly placed inside. As soon as the outside air touches them, the objects seem to finally breathe and swell up in size. Frocks. Dresses. Sweaters. His daughter's childhood belongings. And on top of everything is a piece of paper that has turned yellow with age. A report for sperm count that clearly states: zero.

Gunjan sir recoils, straightens up and runs back. He must get back to the highway by all means necessary. He rushes up the stairs he had taken a while ago. Somehow, he manages to clamber up to the phone booth, pushing down the plank to shut the passageway. Attempting to escape the booth, he realizes the door can't be opened. Somehow he's been locked from outside.

Isn't there a police station nearby? Can he not call for help? What is this place? He glances at the fat book covered with newspaper—the directory. Not as thick a book as it generally is but fat enough. All the important numbers will surely be there. He skims through the pages and finds them packed with lines of English prose. Which book is this? As he turns back to the title page, his breath catches in his throat. *Remembrance of Things Past.* Marcel Proust. His eyes glaze over and he can feel himself getting dizzy. Somehow or the other he must escape this suffocating booth.

But that is not to be. As he bangs on the glass door, strangely the glass walls of the phone booth begin to get concealed by wooden planks. No one is visible outside, just an unknown force loudly hammering nails into the wooden boards over the glass walls. No matter how much he fights, there is nothing he can do. In no time, the booth is transformed into a coffin. He senses it tilting, as if people have lifted it up on their shoulders and begun to move.

'*Bolo Hori, Hori bol.*' Gunjan can hear the funerary chants. 'Chant Hari's name, Hari's name we chant.' There, he can hear it again. He senses he does not have much time left. He can feel himself choking up. The cortege comes to a sudden halt. The lid of the coffin, what was a phone booth until a little while ago, bursts open. For a moment, Gunjan glances up at the open sky, bright and blue. He can feel the sunlight on his face, quite harsh. But not for long. Unexpectedly, the face of a young girl appears; she leans inside towards his chest. He knows the face well. With her back to the sun, it is a little difficult to see her, but Gunjan can still recognize her. Asmita. For an instant, she stares at him with an odd expression. Then she lays down a folded piece of cloth on his chest.

'I had your handkerchief with me, Sir. I came to give it back to you.'

It has taken Abanish a long walk from their house to reach this slum. It is quite late now; he had set out in the evening without anticipating that it might take so long. He can somewhat recall crossing a wood, a marsh and fields after fields, he can still visualize them. And now here lies the slum in front of him. Their domestic help has not been coming to work for three days, so he had set out to check on her. Things have been difficult at home.

Seeing the slum in the distance, Abanish hastens towards it. However, his legs seem to have no strength left in them, he has to drag them forward with much effort. He is thirsty. He can see a hilly settlement, bathed in moonlight. There is not much by way of streetlights. Through the tiny box windows of the tiled homes, flickering lights from lamps can be seen. At various places by the road, food is being prepared on open wood-fire ovens, their reddish glow spreading in the air as colour. There is no other light anywhere. Moonlight seems to have sprung upon the land and drawn a glowing frontier over the neighbourhood, spread evenly from the rows of mountains in the distance to the rooftops of the rows of houses nearby. On the path through the slum, boulders of different sizes are strewn around, stray ones as well as in heaps.

There is a cold air blowing. Abanish did not think he would need a shawl, he had set out early evening right after getting back from work. It is very cold now. He is coming here after a long time. Some of the mountains seem new to him, he cannot make sense of the way and he cannot find the house either. All the houses look similar, it is difficult to decide which door to knock on. However, he has to find the right house soon because it is very late, and he would need to cross all those fields, marshes and woods to get back. Will it be dawn by then? Further ahead, he notices an old woman sitting at the entrance of one of the lamp-lit homes. Going up to her, he enquires, 'Do you know where Sabita lives?'

The woman was kneading dough. The oven in front of her has just been lit, perhaps she was in the middle of making rotis for dinner. She glances up from the task, her manner absolutely still. In the dim glow of the silvery moonlight and the golden fire of the oven, Abanish sees that the woman does not have eyes. In their place is a pair of gaping hollows. A little unsettled, he moves a little closer. By now, other people have begun to gather around him. A little girl from one of the homes, older people from another, a young boy, many approach him with obvious curiosity. Abanish knows they are surrounding him because he is an outsider.

He clears his throat and repeats the question in a softer voice. 'Actually, I was looking for Sabita. Can anyone of you show me to her house?'

All of a sudden, the onlookers light the little lamps they are holding and raise them closer to their faces. Abanish realizes none of them have eyes. Instead, all of them have the same two hollows for sockets. And all of them are trying, with perfect coordination, to surround him. Despite the cold breeze, he begins to break out into a sweat.

As he tries to recede, a loud male voice rings out from a house in the distance. 'Are you looking for Sabita?'

The crowd surrounding Abanish splits into two, giving way for him to pass. He walks up to the source of the voice, a little tiled shanty at the far end of the slum. A middle-aged man stands at the door holding the pale curtains aside; he has no eyes either. As Abanish tries to think how he ended up in this slum of only visionless people, the man speaks again. 'What is it? Where are you from? Why are you looking for Sabita?'

The voice and manner of talking seems exactly like Tarun Pyke, their union leader. But this man is not Tarun.

'Sabita works as a help in our house. She has not been to work in three days, so I came to check on her. Is she unwell?'

The man seems to measure him up with those sightless caverns in place of his eyes. Then he speaks again. 'Sabita will not be going to work any more.'

'What? Why? Is everything okay?'

Letting the curtain drop, the man replies as he turns to go inside, 'I told you, she won't be going to work any more. She was run over by a train day before yesterday.'

Abanish stands there in shocked silence. Then, as he turns around to start for home, he finds the entire slum gone, simply vanished. Instead, he is on some hilly terrain with mountains in the distance, and all around him, instead of rocks and boulders are strewn parts of printing machines. A paddle here, some cartridges there, plates or sets of metallic types, all rusty and covered in cobwebs as if they have been lying here since ages. In the middle of all this is a table with chairs on either side, with the moonlight over it resembling a spotlight. On the table is a pair of glasses with a peg of whiskey in each. In one of the chairs, the one facing him, is Suhrid. Suhrid Dasgupta.

Like an automaton, Abanish walks up to the table, pulls the second chair to sit and takes a sip from the neat peg of whiskey. The liquid burns his throat. Scrunching his eyes, he sets down the glass.

'Reduce your drinking, Abanish-da. I am not asking you to quit, just scale down a little. It's becoming too much these days.'

Abanish keeps staring at Suhrid. Because of the moonlight falling over his head, the younger man's tousled hair resembles a field of silvery grain. But his face is dark, only his eyes seem to be burning. Seeing him silent, Suhrid goes on. 'Swear on my head, you will reduce the drinking.'

'You know I don't believe in such things.'

In response, Suhrid raises his arms, grabs hold of his own head right below the neck with both hands and forcefully pries his head off his shoulders. Blood begins to gush out, staining his shirt, the tablecloth and the moonlight, red. Suhrid calmly lays down his decapitated head on the table. As Abanish stares in disbelief at the bloody head in front of him, Suhrid's torso gets up from his chair, seemingly writhes in pain for a moment and then, with a couple of somersaults, leaps into the darkness and disappears. Immediately, the head on the table looks at Abanish directly and speaks. 'Do you believe me now? Swear on my head.'

16

There they are by the Window
Head resting on their hands
Flowers sprinkled over their lap
A garland they forgot to string
There they are by the Window.

Anuja leans lightly against the parapet in one corner of the roof as she sings, her voice measured and refined. Looking at the way she holds her slim, petite frame as it lightly grazes the corner wall, to Pushkar it is reminiscent of how the fingers of a bereaved family member linger over the deceased before they vanish in flames. They are on the roof of Nirban's house, but this evening the place belongs to all of them. They had decided that before submitting the manuscript to Pradip-da they would get together and have a final meeting to discuss the things that still needed taking care of. They have very little time at hand. It is all happening so fast and yet all of them are excited about this project. They know there will be mistakes galore but none of them want to pass up on the sheer experience of it. The more immediate agenda for the meeting is the matter of collecting their individual contributions for the publication of the book. Pradip-da did not ask for an advance, he never does, but this is a big venture and some money must be given to him. Therefore, they decided to extend this week's Sunday meet until night and use to the opportunity as well as the rooftop as an excuse for an evening potluck. Nirban is in charge of the chicken and rice. Besides, there is spicy dum aloo, green pea kachori, fish fry, and pumpkin and potatoes sautéed in spices. Due to Sabita's absence from work, Pushkar's mother has had to cook these past few days. Despite her hectic music classes, she managed to prepare egg curry for about eight people.

There is a single lantern in one corner of the roof, totally unnecessary given the moonlit night, but burning to the best of its ability. They were in the middle of a discussion when Manideepa had interrupted the conversation. 'I cannot stand these meetings and accounts any more. We are having a picnic. Let's think about all that later. Can we not have some music right now?'

Nirban had laughed. Everyone knew this fond telling-off was meant especially for the editor. Nirban is usually very strict about these matters, so there are no chances of error. So today he had begun as usual, but he had to accept Manideepa's plea and relent. None of them knew when they were all going to be able to meet again, on a rooftop like this in such weather and in this kind of light.

'What have all of you named your books? I have not heard them yet,' Nirban enquired.

'*Spiderwebs and the Death of God* .'

'*Birth of a Fairy Tale.*'

'*Poor, Lonesome Cloud* .'

'*Sometimes I Think about You.*'

'*O Ship, Body's Illusion.*'

One by one they had announced their titles on this long rooftop awash with moonlight. A mat was spread on the floor and steaming tea arrived. Steam mixed with moonlight looks like mist, Pushkar could never have known.

'Fantastic names,' Nirban said, 'Mine is *Wretched Puppets of a Dead City*. Yours?'

It was clear to everyone the question was meant for Pushkar, who was leaning against the parapet and listening intently but not speaking a word.

'I have not thought of one. I will think of one very soon.'

'Don't take too much time. We have to release the fliers with all the names, remember that.'

Nirban's reminder had been a cue for Khurshid's next question. 'So, we have to name the complete book as well, right? Have any of you thought of anything?'

The fact that no one had considered this question until then became obvious at once as they looked at each other awkwardly. Only the determined smile on Nirban's face, revealed in the dim light of the lantern, assured them he had thought of something.

'No matter how much you abuse the editor, he does the most work. I have thought of one, see if you like it . . .'

Before Nirban could finish his sentence, Manideepa's left hand had shot up and covered his mouth.

'Not one more word about work. If we let him, this editor will spend the entire night with all this. Names, etc. First a song. Have any of you heard Anu sing? I'm asking every one of you except one particular person.'

Four things had happened simultaneously with these loudly spoken words. As she removed her hand, Nirban had smiled and relented. 'Alright.' Some of the others burst out with a 'No, we have not heard her sing'. Anuroop gave a shy smile and Anuja, fiddling with her dupatta, seemed to recoil a bit. Never much of a talker, Anuja hardly looks people in the eye. The best way to sense her presence is to note an extra shadow or some added silence in a room. Therefore, everyone understood the public revelation that she could sing would obviously make her further uncomfortable. But Manideepa is too determined a person to let go of something easily. Anuja did try to skirt the issue initially, but eventually she had to give in to the consensus. Almost like a leaf, it seemed to Pushkar, in a tree where the other leaves have robbed her of her right to be alone.

Anuja had got up and walked to the parapet at the far end. Leaning against it, turning her face away from the others in way that made the moonlight cast a silvery outline around her, she had begun to sing in a refined and measured voice, almost as if she were singing to herself. A little more light of the moon, gleaming on the trail of her dupatta, among the stray locks of her hair, the dial of her wristwatch, the pin on the shoulder of her kurta . . .

There they are by the Window
Head resting on their hands
Flowers sprinkled over their lap
A garland they forgot to string
There they are by the Window.

Khamaj. The raag strikes his ear with the refrain's first stanza. This is how he senses the form of a song, recognizes it, just like this. Perhaps not always, but most of the time. He has never read the lyrics of this song by Rabindranath Tagore, only heard it playing a couple of times. This is not a song he has played on loop like many others. Just as the lyrics seek to create a mood of concealment, the fate of the song has not managed to escape it either. The girl sitting by the window, so listless that the flowers lie abandoned on her lap, forgotten to be woven into a garland. She must be thinking of someone, isn't she? Someone long gone. Or someone yet to arrive. Either separation or anticipation, the key ingredients of the song's music and its lyrics. Both require seclusion. Neither is possible to achieve in front of others, in a crowd. So, this girl sits by a quiet window alongside her unruly listless heart. But it is not just any window, not the regular windows they talk about at random. She is sitting by a Window. With the capitalized letter she has stretched it out, made it as timeless as her wait. Pushkar is instantly reminded of the twin window-sisters in his room. When they are half-open, they are simply windows. However, when Pushkar throws open the light shutters completely, hoping for a better view or some breeze, the two sisters spread their square wooden wings right in the middle of the narrow alley of their neighbourhood.

They become complete, untainted and free. From a window, they transform into a Window. Pushkar can acknowledge that this is not merely a simple change of the alphabet. Rather, it is a representation of endless possibilities which motivates an anxious window somewhere to transform into a Window. In addition, since this Window opens to the notes of Khamaj, its shutters must be rather wide. Pushkar can perfectly visualize the song in this manner. He can envision Anuja as well, the perfect agent for the song, possessing all the components necessary to become the aforementioned girl. Pushkar cannot imagine how someone might miss *seeing* such a visual song.

He can perceive the song's air of lightness as well, the clear notes of Khamaj, at least till the first stanza. *Ga Ma Pa Dha Ni Sa*. How the melody rises, like going up a flight of stairs to reach the roof, like all of them had done when coming here. In this case, it is just the raag that ascends. Songs always strike Pushkar's ears just like this. Since he was a child, he has heard the movements of so many raags that he cannot even remember when he wrapped them all around his limbs and his body. He never had to understand them separately or think about them or know them. He only had to listen, to submit his ears and his soul to them. In return, they graced him with their form, their names, so he would never lose his way in the realm of music. So that no matter the road, the turn, the alley or the forest, the way would not be unfamiliar to him. So, he can recognize the nature of those paths, their forms and their names. Music submits itself to him by way of those raags.

Just as he can visualize it now. This song, pushing open the sturdy gates of Khamaj, walking towards him. Past the open door, Pushkar can see light, the light of the raag that aids him in translating the entire song. Hidden from sight, somewhere in the distance, is another song playing, another voice is heard. Ustad Amir Khan saab singing, '*Piya ke awan kin sunat khabariya, lag rahi jau re najariya*' [Awaiting news of my love's arrival, I can barely remain awake]. Also in Khamaj, a thumri. On this stunning moonlit rooftop, the two songs, buoyant on the flow of the same raag, seem to mingle with each other. And the scene? No matter how different the two songs are in their language and manner of singing, when it comes to the scene, is it not the same? A girl sits gazing at the window, waiting for news of her lover's arrival. Alone, lovelorn. From Amir Khan's voice the girl walks to Anuja's and then walks back again. From Hindi she travels to Rabindranath Tagore's Bengali and then back to Hindi again. Actually, there is only one terrace. Of moonlight. Of anticipation. Of Khamaj. That is where she is walks back and forth, all by herself. Pushkar closes his eyes and sees it clearly. When he opens his eyes again, in place of Anuja, he can see that girl from the songs. Women who wander through songs must all surely look like this.

As Pushkar wonders whether the best course of action after such a song is for all of them to head home, Nirban speaks out. 'Really! You are such a fabulous singer, and we did not even know. It's a shame!'

'I deserve the thanks, Mr Editor. This is why you must not think only about work all the time. Shouldn't you have known about this?'

As Manideepa replies with a laugh, Anuja stands in the corner against the parapet. It seems to Pushkar there can be two possible reasons why. Either she has not yet come out of the after-effects of the song, or the figure standing there is someone else and Anuja is no longer here with them.

'Alright, now all of you drop your contributions in this box. Let's count some money under the moonlight.'

Pushkar turns around and sees Nirban has opened a small tin suitcase, the kind they used to carry to school as children, and placed it on the mat. The moonlight never falls the same way on tin as it does on a song. One after the other everyone takes out money from their pockets and wallets and puts it in the box. In front of them all Pushkar is forced to admit, 'Please give me a bit of time. It will be a little easier if Dad's bonus comes through—'

Nirban stops him mid-sentence. 'That's alright. There is no hurry. Let me give your share. You return the money when you can. That's fine, right?'

Pushkar's face dips a little, in diffidence and gratitude.

'I have thought of a name for the book. Tell me what you think. *Inscriptions*. We cannot change it once it's finalized. So, let me know right now.'

A few glances darting here and there, smiles of satisfaction all around. It's perfect. The choice is unanimous. Nirban speaks again.

'See, we can brainstorm and give the book a fancy and complicated name, but what's the point? Instead, let the name stand for who we are. We don't know where we will be in the next few years. When someone picks up the book years later, dusts off the pages and reads through it, it will just be like discovering an ancient language. Think about it . . . To some future reader, our forthcoming book will be an inscription of the past. They will decode it and come to know us through our words . . .'

Satisfied that no one has any reason to disagree, he continues. 'However, one of us must work on the cover.

If we hire a professional artist, it will be expensive, we cannot afford it. Who here can draw?'

Three hands go up in the moonlight: Manideepa, Saswata and Pushkar.

'Great! You have seven days. Prepare an artwork and show it to me. We will use the best one.'

A little while after this, following a couple more things, everyone steps downstairs one by one to set the table for dinner. As Nirban gathers up the mat and puts out the lantern, a female figure detaches herself from her spot in the corner of the roof and seemingly emerges from the reverie of a song. Anuja. The loud voices of the others can be heard fading past the first floor. Anuja rummages in her bag and pulls something out. Holding it in her fist, she extends it to Nirban.

'Keep this. It will make me happy.'

Hearing a spontaneous full sentence from her, Nirban glances at her in surprise. Not at her face but at her outstretched palm. There is a necklace in her hand. The colour of gold does not change much under moonlight, so it is easy for Nirban to tell.

'What is this? Why are you giving me your necklace?'

'Please keep it.'

'How can I? And why?'

'Would you have taken my poetry?'

'Of course, I would have.'

'Then? Is this more valuable than poetry?'

'Oh, I did not say that! But what's the need for this?'

'There is, Nirban. You are doing a lot of this alone, you are doing it for everyone. That is why you are the editor, the driving force behind the journal. I do not contribute in any way. I do not write, do not check proofs or go to the press.

Still, I have formed a connection with all of you in this time. If you take this, I will know I have a part in your book too, that I have a share. That I have been on this journey with you. I know it is a tiny contribution, perhaps too crude, but I do not possess the gift of letters. Does that mean you will not consider me a part of this? Do you think that is fair? Don't worry. This is between us. No one will ever know. However, as you were saying, when many years later these inscriptions are deciphered, I, too, will take joy in the knowledge that I have been a part of it all. The very thought gives me comfort and joy. Do not take that away from me please.'

Nirban gazes at her for a long time. Then something shiny like the moonlight, slender and of the colour of molten gold, passes from one hand to another. He fondly draws a furrow in her hair, saying, 'Now I get it.'

'What?'

Nirban stares at her again for a while.

'How you can sing like that.'

17

Pushkar stays up at night, night after night. His head bends over his small desk, beneath the table lamp. The small yellow light floods his thick head of hair. He stays up, night after night. He stays awake staring at the poems copied on the long, full-scape ruled pages. Everything else on the table has been pushed to the sides. Bent over the manuscript spread on the table he stays awake. Sometimes he quietly stares at his words, at times he changes a word here and there in red ink. But he does not sleep, he stays awake amid pieces of art paper and his colours. He scribbles, erases them, scribbles over them again. Sometimes he comes and sits by the window to observe the night outside. There is no snow, no rain, only the window. His chin resting on his hands for hours, he sits until dawn. Then in the morning he falls asleep, dishevelled, on his untidy bed. There are stains of red ink all over his body, marks of healing. He checks and rechecks the proofs of the poems, repairs them, goes through them again. He traces his own words with his fingers. Eventually he has to get spectacles, something he has never needed before. Alongside the cockroach-coloured frame arrives the third set of edits— one last chance. A close observation of his face reveals he is no longer himself, that he is trying to transform into a book. It is his own proofs that he has been repairing, night after night.

Time   Goes   By

Things bought for the wedding pile up in Asmita's room. She returns home from college to stand in one corner of her room and stare at everything. It is suffocating for her, it makes her want to weep. Her bed, clothing rack, wardrobe, dressing table—she can recognize nothing. Sarees after sarees pile up on her bed, make-up items jostle for space on the dressing table. The date of her wedding is fixed, her mother comes by to show her the text and design of the invite. Asmita stares at it without saying anything, cannot bring herself to. From one evening to the next, new things continue to crowd her room. The room, however, continues to grow old. Entire days she spends with her hands resting on the wall or standing for hours with her back against it. She does not wish to leave this room at all. One day, she climbs up to the terrace at dusk by herself. Making her way through the rows and rows of clothes drying in the sun, she goes and stands by the parapet. She opens a thin volume of poetry. Tracing the letters of a page with a feather stuck in it, she gently brushes them with her fingers, showering them with love. One day she gets into the bathroom, closes the door behind her and stands underneath the shower fully dressed. The rushing water begins to soak her as she weeps. Water trickles down the folds of her wet salwar-kurta.

Asmita covers her face with her hands, concealing herself, but she is not entirely sure who it is she wishes to hide from.

Time   Goes   By

Abanish is seen standing outside his office. On the footpath opposite the building, under the scorching sun. Above him, high above, the light from his office is visible through the square glass windows even during the day. Writing, composing, proofreading, printing, the work never stops. Abanish can hear the sounds from below, but on certain days he cannot bring himself to enter the building. In fear, in shame. In the evening, he heads to the bar with the low lights and cheap decor, alone. Against the tawdry light his face appears dark. He orders four pegs of whiskey, one after the other. Then he takes out stacks of papers from his backpack and places them in front of him. Poetry, his own. Servers come and go, the other patrons regard him curiously. But he sits staring at the papers. When at work, he paces up and down the stairs. At night, he goes and stands where the tramlines intersect, with him at the centre, the city around him, the traffic, the lights, everything shooting past rapidly. As if they have all decided to leave him to his own devices. His eyes, hidden behind his glasses, are visible from up close. They look like they are about to shut, they wish to. Abanish gets on trams that do not ply towards his locality, their brief yellow lights dot his tousled salt-and-pepper hair. A family can be seen lighting a wood-fire oven by the road. A traffic constable plops down in a bus-stand seat, exhausted. The candy-seller gets off the metro, his jar awash with dark colours—red, green and yellow. Signals. Trams grind to a halt. Suddenly, Abanish feels like throwing up. By the road, on a tall balcony, two women casually burst into laughter.

Time   Goes   By

The professor goes on teaching, writing equations on the board. During such times, Khurshid takes out the proofs hidden within his course books and goes through them. The shapes of his poems appear before his eyes. The professor notices, Khurshid smiles through the scolding. It is daylight outside the window. Soutak and Simanta climb the steps of Coffee House, they remain occupied in conversations and debates. The afternoon sunlight streams past the long windows on to their table as a pair of timeworn hands sets down two cups of infusion in front of them. Each of them takes out a fresh bunch of proofs from their bags as they lean over each other's work. Anuroop steps out of his tuition classes on to an old lane in north Kolkata. At the crossing he stops a man selling *ghoti gorom*, a spiced mix of gram-flour munchies, fresh and warm, and buys some. A dog in the distance draws his attention and he smiles at it. The ghoti gorom-seller takes the money and walks away with a salute. Simanta walks into Pradip-da's press in a tearing hurry. The latter blasts him but nonetheless hands over an envelope. One evening, Nirban visits Saswata. In the front yard of his house, covered in blue tarpaulin, idols are being sculpted. The yard is lit by a few bulbs hanging from the ceiling. Nirban stands alone among the crowd of effigies, watching Saswata skilfully work the clay on one of his hands. Saswata notices this and is taken back, they both smile. Saswata goes inside the house and comes back with three hundred rupees. Anuja is alone in her room on the second floor. She takes a book out of the shelf and begins to read. *Don Quixote*. She leans in and takes a whiff of the page. A slight smile appears in one corner of her lips.

Time   Goes   By

Ishita comes out of the shower and walks up to her desk. It usually remains closed, full of old things. Sunlight gleams on the red floors of their rented house. She opens the desk, and taking out an album, very carefully wipes the dust off the cover with her hands. The album opens to reveal a tattered cellophane page, a hazy photograph behind it held by photo corners. Ishita flips through the album. They are mostly pictures of when she was a child, singing on stage with her father, or on the roof with her parents, with Dada. It has her wedding photos too. She places her hand on them once and turns the page. The last photo she stops at is from her father's funeral. She stares at his serene face for a moment, encircled in wreaths of flowers, and then tucks away the album. From another compartment in the desk she takes out a few cassettes. Ninety minutes worth of recorded blank cassettes. She tries to read the fading letters written on the narrow label of the cassette. *Kausi-Kanada*, Lucknow, 1983; *Puriya Kalyan, Desh thumri*, Bombay, 1980; *Yaman, Bageshri, Meera's bhajans*, Moscow, 1987. She keeps staring at them for a long time. That very moment, Pritha shuts the door of her room. It is late. Having finished all her chores, she switches on the small light in her room and picks up her tanpura. She places her fingers on the four strings.

Time   Goes   By

Abhijit stops by the grocery store in their neighbourhood on his way back home. He buys a few things and pays for them. Then he turns away to head home without picking them up. The shopkeeper yells after him, but he pays no heed. He walks into his room and sits quietly. Does not change, does not take off his bag or his shoes. His mother brings in some mixed moori with tea. Patting her son fondly on his head, she leaves. The bathroom light goes on, then off, then on again. He finds himself standing in a queue at the post office. Then sitting in class in college. Lying on the ground in a park by the road. The sunlight brightens and then dims. He sits in his tiny balcony with his back to the wall. He pushes a Suman Chattopadhyay cassette into the recorder next to him but does not switch it on. While cleaning his table in the morning he comes across a book of poems. Slender and old. He considers it for a moment. He sits with his friends in class. All around him conversations rage. Abhijit and Pushkar walk by the lake, both staring at the ground, neither of them uttering a word. They catch a fleeting glimpse of the balloon-seller, the phuchka vendor, the rickshaw-puller. A flash of a turning wheel, force, movement. Abhijit lies down on his bed at night and flicks off the nightlight. Through the window moonlight trickles in, forming bars of a prison across his face.

Time   Goes   By

Gunjan takes classes. He walks down corridors. He sits in the teachers' room and goes through answer scripts.

He stops by students at the corner of the stairs and talks to them. His gestures, the movement of his lips, the frames of his glasses, everything is visible up close. He walks up to the roof of the college and stands there. Alone. In the distance the skyline of Kolkata comes into view, the Howrah Bridge, the second Hooghly River Bridge. A cigarette butt is stubbed out on the ledge of the roof, the steam dissipates into the air. He visits the market in the evening. Bulbs hanging by threadbare strings from the roof of the shop frames cast their light on the vegetables and the fish. Spinach, beet, peas, eggplants, pointed gourds, ridged gourds, bell peppers, tomatoes, all laid out next to each other. The vendor sprinkles water on them. Gunjan asks him to weigh a few things. Fish. Rohu, katla, snapper, Indian salmon, tilapia, butterfish, mullet, mystus, Indian featherback, wallago catfish—all spread out next to each other. Gunjan checks the gills and his fingers come away stained with blood. They are fresh. He unlocks the door and walks into his house. He takes out a bottle of water from the fridge and takes a few swigs. His face appears cold and placid in the light of the fridge. He puts some food inside the microwave to heat it up. The glow instantly warms up his face. He stands by the window. The lamp post undulates and looks fluid as it casts its reflection on the water of the pond outside. He lights up a cigarette and lets out a puff of smoke. Then he pulls out a thick book from a shelf on the bookcase. *Remembrance of Things Past.* He leafs through the pages, stops, turns a few more, stops. Then he sits down at his desk and pulling out his pad begins to write. His pen moves with a grating sound on the fresh page. In a city far away, a little girl wakes up, early in the morning. She glances outside

her window and finds mist. She cuddles the teddy bear next
to her and stares outside quietly for a while. Then she cuddles
the teddy bear one more time.

Time   Goes   By

Saheli is on a vacation with her parents and older brother.
She is seated by the window, her face pressed against the bars
of the train window. Half her face is lit up in the sunlight.
She smiles. Slightly, but it is a smile nonetheless. Softly so
no one understands. In her hotel room she sets down her
luggage and throws open the windows. The wispy white
curtains blow in the wind and graze her face. She leans out
the window and stares out into the distance. She smiles
again. One can see in her eyes that the sea is nearby. Waves
crashing, foam scattering on the shore, the wild raging sea
whose water transforms from grey to greenish to light blue.
The wind makes her flowing hair billow around her. She
tries to contain them with her slender fingers. Evening sets
in early by the sea. Lights come on in the shops as people
make their way from the beach after a day of bathing in the
water. Two kids throw a glowing yo-yo into the receding
waves and then race to retrieve it. Saheli's parents lounge
under a beach umbrella. It is windy. She starts walking along
the shoreline, dressed in a white skirt with printed flowers
and a black t-shirt. Waves roll in and wash her feet. She
kneels and writes something on the wet sand. Then she rubs
it out and keeps walking. Lights are visible in the trawlers in
the distance. She buys a packet of peanuts and settles down
on the sand. She cracks open a shell with her fingers and

looks at the two nuts settled side by side. She smiles again, very softly. The wind blows again.

Time

Goes

By

As time goes by, against the backdrop of these flickering scenes, the strains of Ustad Ali Akbar Khan's sarod can be heard. Raag Mishra Kafi. The *alap*, the *jor*, the *jhala*, then the *gath*, the set tune. First the Madhalaya Rupak, then the Drut-Teentaal.

When read a second time, alongside the same sense of passing time and the exact same scenes, one can hear Schubert's 'Fantasia in F minor', on a piano.

The third time there is just silence.

18

The room has a very tall ceiling, like from colonial times. None of the walls are visible, but the floors are made of antique wood. Pushkar can clearly see the light from the table lamp glistening off the deep colonial varnish on the wood. The room is massive. There is a tall door at the far end, its wooden shutters closed. This side, where Pushkar is seated, there is another door like that, but this one is open. He has never seen this room before, but now here he is, along with his desk and chair. He is in one corner of the room, sitting with his elbows resting on his desk. All the books have been pushed aside and he is drawing a map on a large sheet of cartridge paper, although even he cannot tell what map it is.

The light of the lamp spills over on to the bright white paper, pens of various colours scattered on it. In the low light, he can also make out his surroundings, the floor, the walls and the ceiling. There is no other light in the room, but it is quite clear that all the walls are lined with bookshelves from top to bottom. There is not a single empty slot anywhere, it is all packed tightly with books. In the narrow field created by the light, most of the books seem unread to him. Pushkar notices several tanpuras strewn about on the wooden floor. Much to his surprise, not even one of them has any strings. Pushkar is aware of how naked a tanpura without strings looks. It is a shame. And the way they have been left around, one would have to expend a lot of effort to avoid stepping on them. Who left behind so many tanpuras in this room?

Pushkar can overhear a conversation, it is distracting him from drawing his map. At the other end of the room, beside another set of long doors, two people are seated on the floor, talking. Ishita and Abanish. Versions of their past lives. As if they have just stepped out of their wedding album into this room. For a conversation. Not to scream, fight or argue, just to talk. Ishita has her small tanpura near her lap, the one called Chhutki. Pushkar can recognize it from afar. Abanish is on his knees in front of her. Without any light in the room, he can vaguely make out that they are his parents. But their words are absolutely clear, thanks to the woodwork in the room.

'What is this, you have not put the string on yet?'

'How can I do all this by myself? You spend the entire day at work. I have begun, let me do the small one first.'

'There was a union meeting. I was waiting just like that.'

'You want some tea? I can barely see in this darkness let alone put this string on.'

'No, that's okay. I had tea outside a while ago. When did the power go? I can't stand this any more. Every single day . . .'

'It's been a while. It's not the power, it's our fuse. Don't you see the other houses have their lights on? Look around for the string for the first note, I can't find it.'

'Let me see . . .'

Abanish searches his pockets and then hands Ishita a rolled coil of string. She unrolls it and tightens the string along the length of the tanpura.

'If it's a daughter, what will you name her? Have you thought about it?' she asks.

'You take care of it, I can't think. Have you come up with any?'

'How about Suha?'

'Beautiful! There is a beautiful rendition by Amir Khan saab. I heard him live, 1963, Mahajati Sadan.'

'I have heard him too, in Lucknow.'

'Yes, that time when you went to perform. Okay, so what if it's a boy?'

'If it's a boy . . . if it's a boy . . .'

She finishes tying the string as she repeats the words unconsciously. She turns the pegs and tightens it. Then a single pluck on the string of the first note and the entire room is flooded with light. Ishita and Abanish look around in astonishment.

'You have again handed me the fuse wire. Now if the tanpura stops, the light will go out again. Who will keep playing this all night?'

Pushkar observes Abanish getting up on his feet, he appears almost thrice the size of what he is. From his end of the room, Abanish directs an angry glance at him.

'Who are you? Have you come to fix the fuse? Can't you see we are talking?'

Unable to think of what to say, Pushkar rushes towards the open door near him and escapes to the next room. As soon as he is inside, he notices the room is covered in undergrowth, like it hasn't been cleared in a long time. In one corner is a little girl standing and combing her hair. It's that lonesome girl from the songs. She does not look at him, intent as she is on combing her hair. With every stroke her hair grows in length, mixing with the weed and the undergrowth. At various points in this room, blue tarpaulin has been hung and there are many unfinished idols of Durga scattered here and there. Bulbs hang by strings suspended from the tall ceiling, bathing the room in a strange glow. Each idol catches the light differently, they each appear a little different from the other. Walking past the idols, Pushkar senses that he is stepping on something as he walks. He tries to see what it is and finds the undergrowth crawling with letters and digits of a keyboard, all the letters of the English alphabet, the digits and numerous stars. They are not still; they move about in the underbrush like spirited insects.

Pushkar finds Pradip-da, bent over very low, searching through the weed. His face is sweaty, the shirt on his back soaked through. Noticing him, Pradip-da straightens up.

'Did you not bring the map? How are you going to get back?'

Pushkar lowers his head. 'I made a mistake.'

'This issue won't come out. How can it happen if you submit so late?'

'Actually, it's just one poem, so I got late with the proofreading. What are you looking for, Pradip-da?'

'What else? The accents,' Pradip-da replies as he leans over again to resume his search.

He suddenly disappears behind a bush and Pushkar walks on ahead. Past one idol after another, beneath the warm, hanging bulbs. A little ahead, he finds Saswata working on an idol, grabbing handfuls of clay from a bucket and gradually giving shape to the deity. But he has not a stitch of clothing on his body; completely naked, he is engrossed in his work as if this is entirely natural. Pushkar begins to feel a little uncomfortable. He is not used to seeing people like this but perhaps it's a little more uncomfortable because it's a man in front of him. Seeing him approach, Saswata smiles but continues working. Without a shred of shame or discomfort.

'Why aren't you wearing any clothes? The door is open, anyone might walk in.'

'Maa brings us food,' Saswata replies as he works the clay. 'We cannot wear clothes until we have clothed her.' He smiles again, this time it looks a little paler. He raises one of the clay-stained cold hands and strokes Pushkar's cheek. 'Whatever you see here, these idols are all for the Pujo edition. Haven't you brought some soil too? Your new soil?'

With this last sentence still ringing in his ears, Pushkar wakes up with a start and sits up in his bed. It is almost dawn. He never wakes up at this hour. His body feels clammy. The pyjama strings seem to have come undone at some point. The fresh, soft, moist light of dawn washes over his waist and legs. He stares at himself fixedly, as if he cannot recognize what he is seeing. He remains like that on the bed for a long time. It's a rainy October morning, it will be Pujo soon. A familiar smell hangs in the air, a familiar mood that makes it clear, even without a calendar, that Pujo is just around the corner.

Sitting on his bed, he thinks about the month and a half that has passed in planning, preparing the manuscript and proofreading it. It is Pujo in twelve days. Their book comes out today. Pradip-da finished work at the press a week ago, today it will be bound. The binders are from College Street and Nirban has asked all of them to gather in front of Coffee House by three so they can pick up the books together. Initially, they had decided on five hundred copies as the first print run. Nevertheless, Nirban, with surprising confidence, increased the number to a thousand. Their book, a thousand copies, who is going to buy them? These questions did not dampen Nirban's spirits, neither did the possibility of a deluge. The clouds have been gathering for the past two days, they are predicting this Pujo to be a washout. Pushkar glances at the sky through whatever view allotted to him through the window. It's clear the light is low not just because it's the crack of dawn, but the sky is darkening as well. But they will get to College Street somehow, through storm or rain. To get their new book. The very first one.

The very thought seems unreal to Pushkar. Perhaps that is why he has woken up so early in the morning. A kind of anxiety bubbles in his throat, like a roach forced into a bottle, trying to fly out in vain. Baba is at his night duty; he will be back in a little while. He is expecting his bonus today. At least five hundred would be a lot of help, he has told Baba already. Baba did not say anything, but he did not refuse either. Pushkar will feel a lot better if he can give them some money today.

It begins to rain, softly. The clouds make it known this will go on all day. Outside Pushkar's window, outside the window of Abanish's office, it begins at the same moment. But different kinds of rain. Because while Pushkar looks out his window happily dreaming of hot tea, Abanish, fresh off a sleepless night, tosses a half-smoked cigarette out the window into the rain. It's washed away by the rain even before the flame has gone out.

'There is no point waiting any longer, Abanish-da. Pack everything up. Whatever pieces you have lying around, anything else on your desk, get everything. People are gradually on their way out.'

Suhrid comes up and stands beside him. He looks just as tired.

'Are you sure?'

'What is the point of lying to ourselves? You know this too. Everyone does. You are afraid to go check the notice board, but all the others have read it. When you were releasing the final copy, for today, Ramesh and Sandip put up the notice. Shut down from today. What they call a lockout.'

Abanish stares at the rain intently and says, 'So today, it was the last copy? Never again? And this paper?'

'I don't know, Abanish-da. The owners are absconding. They have such huge debts in the market. I have no clue what agreement they have come to with the union. These days, it's impossible to judge what is right or wrong. They are all incidents. This too is an incident. If not today, it would have happened tomorrow. We were expecting it but not so soon.'

'The bonus?'

'Forget about all that. There will be no salary and here you are asking about bonus. It looks like the union is fighting for the provident funds and gratuities. There is some fraud there as well, apparently a lot of the money never made it to the accounts. Can you imagine!'

'Where do I go now?'

Abanish turns his face away from the rain and directs the question at Suhrid in such a manner that there is no answer for it.

There is a flurry of activity all around, a kind of miserable urgency. Everyone is preparing to leave, in all probability never to come back again. Some after five, some after eleven, some after twenty-three and some after thirty years of service. Defrauded, crushed, defeated, they are being forced to leave. They leave with their heads hanging low, eyes moist, hands tucked to their sides. Members of the union have gathered downstairs, the rain drowning out their uproar. Pujo is around the corner.

Abanish sits down in his chair, his palms spread over his desk. He remains there. Many people come by, some who give him a supportive pat on the shoulder, a couple of youngsters who come by to touch his feet, but he does not move. Many of his pieces are on the desk: features, book reviews, his own poems. He does not bother to open it. A little later, when the rain recedes, he picks up his jhola and walks out on to the road. It's almost morning.

Once out, he does not look in any direction, as everything has begun to seem gigantic to him. The houses all around seem to have grown tenfold; the early morning tram that hurtles past him resembles an enormous prehistoric snake as it makes the road beneath it rumble. The transport, the houses, the markets, everything looks like they have grown overnight, becoming taller and wider. Somehow he manages to pack himself into a bus, a huge one. By the time he disembarks near the crossing of his neighbourhood, he can barely recognize anything around him. Everything has grown to monstrous proportions in just a night. Nonetheless, trying to recall memories of previous nights, he sets out towards home as he tries to ward off the monstrous shops, markets, houses, bridges, advertisements, pharmacies and mills pursuing him with gaping maws, ready to swallow him up.

He walks as Pushkar gets up to make himself some tea.

He walks as it rains heavily.

He walks, forgetting to take out his umbrella.

He walks as Pushkar steps out on to the veranda of their rented house.

He walks just as a torrential downpour starts.

Abanish keeps walking. Sometime later, from the veranda, Pushkar notices his father at the mouth of the alley. Bent over, his kurta and pyjama soaked through, somehow trudging along. The bag hanging from his shoulder looks like it wants to give in to its weight and fall to the ground. He still keeps walking. Placing the cup near the railing, Pushkar advances a little in his direction. He is surprised to find that the more his father approaches the house, the more he seems to shrink. With every step his height and proportions diminish. By the time Abanish reaches the main door and finds himself face to face with Pushkar, he has shrunk ten times his size. Pushkar lowers his head, his Baba appears somewhere near his feet. As if it is not his father but a miniature version of him. Does Baba not exist in his actual size anywhere? Neither in dreams, nor in reality? He glances at his father again, head lowered, standing huddled up near his feet, quietly.

His shrunken Baba.

Soaked to the bone.

Without salary or a bonus.

Locked out.

His unemployed, discarded and exhausted father.

Nothing but a toy.

Pushkar watches him for a long time. Then he kneels and picks Baba up on his palm.

19

Do you know, as a child, I had an immense fascination for toys? Back then there were no video games, no games in phones. Toys were a lot different. We played sports in the fields of course. But there were toy cars, Chinese checkers and bagatelle as well, they captivated me. When did this begin? Back when we were children some of my friends had these toys. Colourful cars, toy trains, so much more! Their parents used to buy them toys from time to time. We did not have a single one of such toys at home. When friends came over, they asked for toys to play with. I used to get very upset. Especially with Baba. He was the sole breadwinner, Ma used to take care of the household. He used to teach English literature in a college, just like me. How much could his salary have been back then? So, we never had anything at home we absolutely did not need. But do you know, Baba used to buy a lot of books. How did I know it was his payday? He would drop by College Street on his way back home and come back with a bunch of books. So many books that he would have to ask the rickshaw-puller for help in unloading them. He was a bookworm. Half his salary went in buying books. Ma used to love books just as much. On most days, at dinner or during tea, I would hear them discussing some novel or an essay they had both just read.

Baba used to buy me books as well; money never came in the way. From Russian folk tales to stories of Panchatantra, from editions of the Mahabharata for young adults to hunting tales, from Leela Majumdar to Rudyard Kipling. Everything. He was happy buying me books and he would also enquire from time to time if I had read them. I developed this love for books quite early on. But on one particular birthday, I ended up demanding a toy from him. A train set where the engines let out smoke. It came with a set of tracks, which had to be arranged in a circle for the wind-up train to go round and round, whistling and emitting smoke. I had seen one at a friend's house and wanted one for myself.

Honestly, I didn't expect Baba to buy it for me. He had turned me down several times earlier. But for some reason, on that occasion, Baba did not refuse. He bought me the train. Exactly the one I wanted. I could not contain my joy at the sight of it. Along with it he also gave me a book, a Bengali translation of the Iliad. It was a translation for children. Baba explained to me who Homer was and why the book was considered an epic. I read it in one go, it was fantastic. Then I read it again, and again. I understood this book was different from the ones I had read before. Not that I forgot about the train set. For the next three months I was obsessed with it, would never fail to show it off to my friends. However, eventually I simply lost interest, packed the set up and stored it away for safekeeping. I was seven or eight, perhaps.

Anyway, many years went by after that, almost a decade. I passed my higher secondary exams with more or less good results. My parents were very happy. That evening, we were *waiting for Baba to get back from college. Baba, probably anticipating the news of my results, walked in with a gift. When I saw it neatly wrapped in brown paper, I could figure it was a fat book. Those days, my parents used to give nothing but books as gifts even at weddings and other family functions. This was going to be no different. I touched his feet, he gave me his blessings. I immediately stretched out my hand for the gift. It was an English edition of the Iliad, this one for adults, with annotations. He asked me to finish it in the two months I had until the start of college.*

I had read the book before, but when I started reading it again, it seemed like a totally different text. Perhaps because with age, I, too, had matured. On reading the book the second time it did not appear quite as facile as it had seemed to me before. It seemed new, as if I had not gone through it previously or even if I had, I did not see it in quite the same manner. By then my senses, intelligence and age, all three had matured. This book was not as easy as the previous version either. All combined, it was a novel experience.

One night, Baba came to my room. After some idle conversation he asked me, 'Have you finished reading the book I gave you? How was it this time?' Excitedly, I told him how much I liked it. I remember seeing my perennially serious Baba smile slightly. Then he got up and brought down the boxed-up train set kept on top of my cupboard. He dusted it off and handing it to me, said, 'Switch this on.' I could not argue with him, so I put the plastic tracks together, wound up the train and let it run. It took some time, but it worked perfectly. When it stopped, both of us got up from the bed. He placed his hand on my shoulder and asked, 'So? Was that just as much fun as before?' He smiled and turned to leave.

Baba could teach the most important lessons with the least words, like he did that day. Let me tell you this today, there is no friend more astounding and incredible than a book. Maybe you have heard this before; if you have, then it's not a lie. The same book will come back to you at different times in different forms. And when you reread it, you will feel different as well. You will comprehend how much you have changed in the intervening years as a reader and as a human being. A few years later, if you read the same book again, you will find it telling you different things. This is the joy of reading books. Hence my parents always got me books. They are a kind of treasure that you never run out of, possessing just increment and magnitude.

Baba would often say that everyone must inculcate an interest in the arts. Those who are not artists, those who possess no artistic talents, even they must forge a connection with art, whatever interests them. Every day, no matter what one's profession is. Because art is like medicine, it's like a shield, a weapon. Everyone needs it, everyone should. As a child, I used to see mechanics singing loudly while digging or working on the pipelines. The rickshaw-puller uncle used to have the radio on at full blast while ferrying passengers. The ailing Rama aunty used to read plays, bank clerk Rajani uncle used to take days off to visit Joydeb Kenduli every year to attend the Baul festival. Even Bishu, known by all and sundry as a goon, was seen playing Kishore Kumar songs and bawling. Art can absorb all decay; in exchange, you have to give it your time and your soul.

As a child I had learnt a Tagore song for a school function. 'Aloker ei jhorna dharay dhuiye dao' [*Cleanse us in this cascade of light*]. *What a fun song! I used to sway to the beats and gesticulate as I sung. Listening to it, singing it, gave me immense joy. I don't sing any more. However, when I listen to the song, even today*

I find in it a sense of joy bigger and vaster than any fleeting sense of amusement, bringing tears to my eyes. It's the same song; the words haven't changed, neither has the tune. What has changed are the times, and I have changed as well. So, the song helps me find my new self. A piece of theatre, a film, a painting, a dance, a symphony, these will remain your lifelong companions, your friends. In your entire life, you can rediscover them countless times, just as you can also rediscover yourself.

Read, alright? Read books. Watch films. Go to the theatre. Watch a dance performance. Listen to music. Appreciate paintings and sculptures. Do these things when you are grown up. Otherwise you will never be able to truly know yourself. And when you are old, with grey hair and a trembling voice, and you come to the realization that you never tried to find your true self, it will make you miserable. Do you like being miserable? You don't, do you? So, get to know yourself better as you grow up, as you grow old. In one lifetime, you will come face to face with multiple versions of yourself. You will look at them and wonder in disbelief: is that even me? You may not be able to believe it, but you will know it is definitely you. A new version, different from the previous ones. It's very important you understand this.

If these words seem difficult to you now, then revisit this letter in a few years. Perhaps then you will be able to understand my words in their entirety. I know you will. I have tried explaining it to your mother as well, but I do not know if I have succeeded in doing so. Instead, your mother has always felt I was trying to hide myself behind my books. Not that she is wrong. Books are often like a shelter, a bunker or even a tunnel. They can give you refuge from calamities, troubles, fights, misunderstandings, failures, problems and arguments of the outside world. They give you a place to hide. A place where no one can find you except you yourself. So, whenever your mother has accused me of hiding behind books, I have accepted it. In the beginning that's what I really used to do, hide myself behind a book. However, as time passed, I realized I was not hiding at all; in fact, it was just the opposite. I was discovering a new world and the new version of me that lived in it. Like how a sailor, fleeing war, chances upon an uncharted island.

This is all I had to tell you. This is why I am writing this long letter to you. Have they taught you prisms in physics? If not, then they soon will. A prism is a reflector that can split light passing through it into its seven components. We do not get to see these seven hues naturally; a prism can separate the colours and reveal them to us. To do that, the light needs to be directed through a prism. Art is like such a prism. Our interactions with art can be transformative encounters. When we go through such experiences and emerge on the other side, they often reveal a lot to us about our own selves. In this case, it's not just seven colours, they are numerous. Things we did not know we had in ourselves.

As I write this, I am reminded of another theory of physics. It's an astounding concept, although it has sparked a lot of debate and caused a lot of trouble as well. I must accept that many components of the theory of relativity seem like poetry to me. Perhaps this will sound too romantic, but considering quantum physics, philosophy and poetry, I cannot always make a clear distinction among the three from afar. Not that I know much of any of the three. Yes, as I was saying . . . like a prism I am also reminded of wormholes. In this ever-expanding space, there might be wormholes scattered about in various places. What do they do? They compress space. You will read about all this later, but just to explain it to you, a wormhole is an extraordinary tunnel that can bring two disparate points in space-time together, capable of reducing distances worth a few billion light years to just a few metres. If you can travel from one side of a wormhole to the other, then you will be able to cross over shocking distances, otherwise impossible even in multiple lifetimes, all in the blink of an eye. Some claim that wormholes can even bring two different points of time together because it can twist the shape of time and bring it closer. So, no one knows what will be at the other end of the tunnel, but they are aware that no matter what, it is very far from this end. Although the existence of wormholes is yet to be proven, I believe there is no greater wormhole than art. It is impossible to fathom what distances art can traverse and encapsulate in a novel, a play, a song or a film. What length of time it can twist out of shape and form into a symphony, a painting or a ballet piece, whisking you away from your time to another. A successful work of art is very much like a wormhole. If you travel from one end of it to the other, you will be able to cross incredible distances that would have otherwise seemed impossible.

So, you must always keep walking. Walk through a novel, a film, a symphony, a play. Pass through them, again and again. Because whenever after a long journey you pass through them to the other side, if you raise your head, you will be able to see your own colours. Things no one else can ever show you.

By the time this letter reaches you, you will have no way to reach me or talk to me any more. But you must not be sad, you must not cry. Promise me, alright? Perhaps I will no longer be able to see you even if I close my eyes and wish for it, but you will be able to! See, I am reminded of physics again. They must have taught you the speed of light by now. It travels one lakh eighty-six thousand miles per second. Unbelievable, isn't it? But do you know what travels faster than light? Thoughts. Our imagination. The soul. So, whenever you want to see me, talk to me, you just need to close your eyes. Nothing can stop you. So, don't be sad.

One day you and I will be the same age. That day we will truly become friends. Then you will gradually grow older than me, enough to be my older sister. And finally, when you become a white-haired woman with trembling hands, then in your heart I will be like your son. It's like magic, isn't it? Memory, too, is often like a prism. Even someone who is gone can become many different people in our memories as long as we are willing to dredge the depths for them.

Don't misunderstand me. Not all roads lead far. People walking down shorter roads need to accept it when they reach the journey's end. What else are they supposed to do? My journey ends here. It ended long before, I know, but I was trying to see if it led to any new directions from here. It did not. I have stayed up many a night looking for a way, now I need some sleep. A long, restful sleep, longer than this letter. So please do not ever misunderstand me. In these past few years, on every birthday of yours, I have bought you many books. I never managed to give them to you. They will probably reach you with this letter. I know for sure all your anger will then vanish, if you are even a little angry.

You will be fine, you will become a beautiful person. And keep yourself beautiful on the inside always. Alright? You will see that way even the outside seems beautiful. Love your mother a lot. Your share, and mine as well. And when you think about me a lot, go near the books I am sending you. They will be me. For the rest of your life, it is through them that we will see each other.

Lots of love. Lots. More than I have ever given anyone.

This long-folded letter is left behind on the other side of the closed door, tucked away between pages forty-three and forty-four of a book *For Whom the Bell Tolls*.

Also left behind is a dark house whose open doors and windows let in the yellowish evening light of the lamp post and the chilly October air.

Rows of books remain, lined up on side of the table, a hundred and twenty-three in all. On the first page of almost each book two names are written, the person giving the book and the person it was given to.

Outside the door a newly bought lock remains hanging, its keys kept in the letterbox meant for this apartment.

In the evening, a slender, desolate girl appears in front of the door, hiding a wedding card in her hands, her own wedding's. Finding the door locked, she stands there surprised for a little while. Then she pushes the card through the sliver of space under the door and leaves.

In the sombre room on the other side, on the dark and cold mosaic floor, a dark wedding invitation is left behind.

The girl takes the road by the lake. In just a few paces she finds a rickshaw that picks her up and speeds away.

Perhaps for this reason the girl does not notice the crowd gathered in the western corner of the still and silent lake. Police vans are arriving. There is commotion all around.

A body is being brought up from the water, just as still and silent.

20

If we slowly retrace our steps from this moment, with the chaos by the lake and the body being retrieved from the water, to just a few hours ago when the long letter was being written, we might catch a glimpse of what else was happening at that time. As the letter is being written, it rains outside. A torrential downpour has covered the entire city. It was barely a drizzle in the morning, but by noon the rain had taken her real form—her hair billowing in the wind as she set about drowning the city in a deluge. College Street, too, could not escape the brutal onslaught. No one would have usually thought of the rain as brutal if not for Pujo, which is just twelve days away. The streamers of light hanging between bamboo poles from the entrance of the neighbourhood to the main road, the ornate pandals being constructed, the beautifully decorated idols being loaded on to trucks, everything is drenched. The entire city is a victim of this cruelty. That is how Pushkar feels about the rain as he takes the shortcut through Medical College to reach Coffee House. It is brutal because the rain reminds him of his father's face that morning—cold and wet.

Brutal because their shiny new book, for which his cover design was unanimously chosen, will surely get wet in this rain. Brutal because even today he wouldn't be able to give Nirban the money for the book as he had promised. He will have to give an explanation and everyone would find out what happened. Tomorrow everyone will know anyway.

Holding the umbrella over his head, Pushkar catches a blurry glimpse of the entrance to Coffee House, glowing in rain-washed fading colours of a few youngsters. The rest have arrived before him, the warmth of their excitement visibly permeating the area. Pushkar hastens and joins the melee. The umbrella is useless, what he needs is shelter. The crowded conversation immediately draws him in.

'Here you are, Pushkar-babu, we were waiting for you.'

'Sorry, I couldn't get a bus.'

'That's okay. None of us have been here long.'

'Didn't Manideepa say she would be joining us after running an errand at Presidency? Where is she?'

'She will be here, I'm sure. What about the book? Is it ready yet?'

'I had called to enquire when I was about to leave. They had said four, so that's ten more minutes.'

'Is everything in order?'

'I think so, or else Pradip-da would have informed us. Pushkar has done a fantastic job on the cover. People are saying good things about it already. Since it's in black and white, it's visually arresting.'

'Pushkar, you said you were out of practice; the cover does not give that impression at all. I had gone to the press the other day. Pradip-da showed me the tracing.'

'But how do we carry the books?'

'That's what I was wondering too. New binding, a thousand copies, it's not a joke. We did not think this through. How do we carry them, Nirban?'

'This is why I am the editor, and you are the subeditors, writers and poets. It has all been arranged.'

'Fine, we accept it, you are the best. Tell us what the arrangements are. So much suspense is not good. There, Manideepa has reached too.'

'I hired a goods vehicle last night. A covered one. It must have reached the press by now. We will carefully load the books and then triumphantly head to my place. There, take whatever number of copies you need; the rest will be kept there. Next Sunday, we will make a list and distribute them. I was thinking of dropping a few copies at Patiram Book Store today, for them to stock, but in this rain . . .'

Before Nirban could finish, Khurshid, Soutak and Manideepa envelop him in a hug. Truly, without some manner of transport how would they have managed to take their books today? No one other than Nirban had thought this through. He glances at his watch; it is five minutes to four, time for them to head to the binder's workshop. Everyone is there except Saswata.

'Isn't Saswata coming?' Nirban asks Anuroop.

'I called him. He won't be able to make it. This is a busy time for him. The idols are being picked up for delivery. They are working through the night. It's impossible for him to get away at this point. If the rain lets up a little, I will drop by his place at night and give him his copy. Now, let's go.'

As they set off, Pushkar can see the narrow old lanes of College Street beginning to melt in the rain. There are tarpaulin coverings everywhere, small bookshops, carts selling pakoras and sugar cane juice, vans carrying reams of paper, the movements of busy people, everything seems to be disintegrating in the rain. His own body feels like it is made of soft clay, like he might dissolve in the water and be washed away before he can get back home.

As the others go ahead excitedly, Pushkar seizes the opportunity to fall in step beside Nirban.

'There is something I need to tell you.'

Looking at Nirban it's abundantly clear that he is not only happy but very proud today. The book has turned out exactly how he had envisioned it. His mood suggests today he feels generous enough to will away the entire city to his friends.

'Tell me, what is it?'

'I don't know how to say this, but . . .'

'Don't hesitate so much, just blurt it out.'

'I couldn't bring the money today. Baba's office has shut down. He got home early this morning, without salary or bonus. He lost his job. So today I . . .'

Nirban stops abruptly in his tracks. The binder's workshop is just a couple of narrow loops away, the smell of freshly printed pages and adhesives hanging in the air makes it evident.

'What are you saying? Why did you come today then?'

'That's fine. What would I have done otherwise? I did not want to stay home any more. But I will soon . . .'

'Don't speak another word about this, Pushkar. Don't think about it either. The fact you are here with me on such a day, nothing is worth more than that. Do you know why you are here?'

'Why?'

'Because of love. This journal, us, writing, you love all of this with your life, it's why you are here even on a day like this. I doubt I would have been able to do this had I been in your place. What more can you give us? Money is not a yardstick by which to measure everything. You have contributed more than all of us put together. Your presence here today means a lot, much more than even you are aware of.'

With these words, Nirban pulls Pushkar into a tight hug. He casts his umbrella aside, leaving it like an upturned bowl in the middle of the road for rainwater to gather in. Their hug lasts a brief, dry instant under Pushkar's umbrella, the one with the broken handle. Sealed packets of books are already being loaded on to the small truck outside the small gate of the factory. In the blinding rain everyone has pitched in to get it done, satisfaction and content evident on their faces, like someone who has just been published for the very first time.

As everyone examines their personal copies, Khurshid hands a copy each to Pushkar and Nirban. There is a stark difference between how one feels before and after holding a new book for the first time. It's a feeling Pushkar is familiar with, a feeling that is quite immeasurable.

Light grey and white letters, uneven and faint, trying to be prominent against black, like a dark and jagged wall unearthed at a dig that has just been touched by sunlight. As if this evidence of an ancient civilization was buried all this while, alongside the history and the script. As if someone has been tending to the stone with the lightest of touches and soft brushstrokes to remove the dirt and make the letters clearer, making them legible. But the words are unknown, they bear no resemblance to any known alphabet system. All except one, made of four familiar characters written in white, among all the other unfamiliar ones. In the Bengali script. *Shilalipi. Inscriptions.*

Below the title, in smaller font, are the names of the poets whose poems make up the collection. Pushkar's cover seems to be awakening, emerging from an endless abyss, from a rain-drenched College Street, buoyed by the kindness of friends. All that is left now is for it to be deciphered.

'You guys are no fun! Even today you will huddle under an umbrella?' Manideepa tosses her umbrella aside on the pitched road of the narrow lane. She raises her arms and begins twirling in the rain. With smiling faces, everyone follows suit, even Pushkar, albeit with some hesitation. They begin embracing each other and dancing in the rain, in a way they have never done before, acutely aware that such a moment will not come their way again.

Simanta rides shotgun, the rest of them stuff themselves along with the boxes of books in the back of the truck. Everything has been wrapped tightly in plastic so that nothing gets wet. Central Avenue in the afternoon, just before Pujo, while it's raining—the traffic is as expected under the circumstances, forcing them to stop from time to time. But none of them seem to notice it as their raucous celebrations mingle with the rain which seems to draw the afternoon out. From one droplet to the next, as numerous new moments form, the slender thread of time seems to lengthen and expand, just like noodles in hot water.

They notice the trucks next to them have people huddled together just like them—youngsters, commotion, audacious laughs. Idols are being ferried from Kumortuli to various pandals. They are also stuck in traffic. Surrounding the transparent plastic-covered idols of the Goddess, young people revel in anticipation of Pujo. This book is their idol, the thought crosses Pushkar's mind. Each of them is taking the idol back to their own altars, from the printer's workshop, the Kumortuli of letters. Just like the bamboo frames, straw, clay, colours and fabric, their book has also been put together using layers of ingredients. Each of them has contributed to it with their own handful of fresh clay. Will someone really unearth it after many years? Inscriptions? The future scares Pushkar. The past too. All he wishes is to live this moment, desperately. Wants to love, everything, as best as he can.

'Will you drop me off at Rashbehari crossing? I have some work,' Pushkar asks Nirban as they cross Park Street.

'What? Won't all of us get together once today? Go after that, please. Although if you must go home . . .'

'No, not home. I have to drop by two other places first. Can I take three copies now? I will pick up the rest tomorrow or day after?'

'That's fine. Alright then, get off at Rashbehari. Be careful, alright? I will get in touch later.'

Rashbehari crossing.

Three books in his wet jhola. New.

Wet batik kurta sticking to his skin.

Side seat of the auto. Rashbehari to Gariahat.

A rainy afternoon settling into dusk.

A boy getting soaked in the rain.

Alone.

Pushkar gets off at Gariahat and starts walking. Somewhat preoccupied. He does not notice if the rain is letting up or getting stronger, whether or not his clothes have dried, whether passers-by are knocking against him or dodging him, whether the shop next to the fruit-seller has utensils or dolls, whether the sky is ash-black or purple-pink. He does not notice any of it. He continues to walk with the books in his bag, single-mindedly, but still distracted. He has to get to someone before anything else, has to give them a copy of the book before anyone else. The rest will come after that. He does not feel like going home, neither does he wish to sit somewhere and read. Down the roads lit up with lights, past the songs blaring through the loudspeakers, evading the haggling of last-minute Pujo shoppers, through a black mass of jostling umbrellas and the aroma of warm parathas and pieces of meat being fried on tawas in the evening, making his way past the customers lining up for rasgullas. Through all of it, there is one thing, a single thing that occupies his mind.

He is in love. He, Pushkar, is in love. A little too much, with everything. He has never felt like this before. But today, while walking from Gariahat to Golpark and then down Southern Avenue, it dawned on him that he is deeply in love with everything that is going on around him. Why, he is not sure. How, he is not sure either. All he knows is that at this very moment, it is love that is becoming his language, his constant recourse. Love. Not just for the people close to him or his writings or his own life. Love for everything. Everything happening around him at this moment, the moving earth, every incident everywhere in the world, the forests, the oceans, the mountains, the plains, the cities, the sky, even the vast outer space beyond earth. He feels his love reaching out to every particle far and wide, like a never-ending stream, like spools of red silk ribbon spilling out of a magician's black top hat, or like the tales of *Jataka*.

He feels powerful. As he walks down this rain-soaked road, he feels like the most powerful person in the world. Because of the love he feels for everything. He does not know where he gets this power from, if it is from poetry, from music or from Saheli, he cannot be sure. Neither does he know since when this ability has been biding its time in his head. All he knows is that he is in love and everything in him is undergoing a transformation. Because he knows, love is like the number zero. Any number, no matter of what magnitude, when multiplied by zero is instantly reduced to zero again. Love has the same power. Just as the zero can consume everything and incorporate it within itself, love can do the same. Anything that encounters love is transformed into it. As he walks, Pushkar can feel this realization radiating from every particle of his body and every corner of his soul.

So, he begins to love with every fibre of his being. Such an afternoon, this rain, a feeling of this kind, he has never experienced something like this before. But this is fun. In this extraordinary joy, he starts to multiply everything with love and they, in turn, begin to transform into love. Poverty, failure, rejection, separation, fatigue, depression, vengeance, slander, hostility, envy, pride, ridicule, conspiracy, compassion, sorrow, pain, agony, wounds, sleeplessness, ailments, evil, success, defeat, violence, boastfulness, politics, lies, injustice, jealousy, regret, malice, misfortune, arrogance, resentment, crime, greed, inactivity, hate, temptation, weakness, dissolution, incapacity, vanity, conceit, egotism, oppression, war, destruction, death. He multiplies each of these with love and sees them transform one after another into love in the blink of an eye. From today this is his shield, this is his weapon, his motto and his remedy. He can transform anything in this time and space into love, in his heart, with his willpower. No matter how forcefully these things come at him, before they can touch him they will be transformed, just as anything that approaches too close to the sun is scorched, ash crumbling from their skin. For Pushkar, that ash too is love. It is also his mode of protest when faced with difficult times. Perhaps people will find this silly, call it an intellectual exercise, so he will not reveal his secret weapon, his motto, to anyone. But he will continue to love everything. There is only one entity to whom he will reveal everything, whom the first copy of the book is intended for, whom he has finally reached after this long walk.

His friend, the milkwood tree, stands tall this October evening, wet from the rain, its intoxicating fragrance in full bloom. Tiny strings of fairy lights dot either side of the road, their light offering up heat to the bunches of white flowers. As one steps into the lane, the smell of these flowers is strong enough to overwhelm the heart, the mind and the body. Pushkar does not know if it is the same with everyone, at least that is how it is with him. He can sense that this fragrance is that of a season. Not autumn or the upcoming dewy season. This heady smell is of love. There has been no season on earth longer and more capacious, and neither will there be any in the future. Today, he cannot talk about all of this with his friend, he must urgently gift it a copy of the book and then rush to see Gunjan sir. The second copy is intended for him. Had Saheli been in town, she would have been the first person he would have gone to see, with his first book, but she is in Puri. So, he will get back home only after seeing Gunjan sir. Things must be despondent at home today. In such a situation all he will be able to offer them is his new book of poems, his first book of poems, hoping that might change something. Even that situation he will try to face with love. He will not be scared. Rather, he will try to deal with their adversity, Ma's pain, Baba's failures, with love, just as he loves them. The two of them were not made up of just music or writing, they consisted of many more things. Today, Pushkar wants to shower attention on it all, multiply all of it with this swift and astonishing current of love washing over him.

He can feel all the years of his life gathering in this new season, alongside his entire future.

He can visualize his past, present and future floating past him slowly, turning the cloudy sky a light pink.

A pair of enormous windows floats by, side by side, rain outside one and snow outside the other.

A huge, reddish-black diary that knows all his secrets.

An immensely long saree, white with a blue border, gigantic enough to cover the entire maidan like an ancient bird flying to its nest at dusk.

A huge book, as large as an aeroplane, named *Remembrance of Things Past*.

A tanpura slightly older than him, called Chhutki, his elder sister.

A pen that resembles a canon, usually tucked away in Baba's pocket.

A black umbrella, resembling a parachute as it floats by.

Pages of handwritten letters, soaring like a flock of carpets.

The title of an essay drifts by, languidly.

The raag Bihag, with its beauty and longing.

A touch glides by, an afternoon's touch, with all its warmth.

Pushkar enters a different season, a different world, a different sky, today, right now.

He takes a book out of his jhola and opens it. His own poem is the fourth one on the list, after three others. But that is not what he turns to. He takes out his pen and on the very first page writes a dedication to his friend, the milkwood tree. He turns another page and makes a small correction in the printer's information on the left. The edition of the book mentions 'October'. He strikes out the month, carefully scribbles something else in its place, places the book near the root of the tree and gracefully turns towards the new world of possibilities that await him. In the old Kolkata that he leaves behind, on a rainy afternoon, a book of poems is left to soak in the rain at the foot of a blossoming milkwood tree. Pushkar's correction glows on its second page—

'First Edition, Love.'

Scan QR code to access the
Penguin Random House India website